Duck Disaster

MOREWELLSON, LTD

Duck Disaster

Copyright © 2022 Vikki Walton

Morewellson, Ltd.
P.O. Box 49726
Colorado Springs, CO 80949

ISBN:
978-1- 950452-35-4 (e-pub)
978-1- 950452-36-1 (standard edition print)
978-1- 950452-37-8 (large print edition)

Front cover illustration: DLR Cover Designs Donna Rogers

Publishing/design services: Wild seas formatting

Editing: Polaris Editing

Duck Disaster

A
BACKYARD FARMING
MYSTERY

VIKKI WALTON

MOREWELLSON, LTD

Chapter One

Anne and Hope were bent over a spreadsheet when Kandi pushed through the door, slamming it behind her.

"Whoa, what's put a bee in your bonnet?" Anne asked. "Your face is as red as your hair."

Kandi plopped into a chair across from the pair, crossing her arms.

"It's the Coles again. She practically screamed at me in front of everyone. They are not happy to hear about the wedding. She said the bed-and-breakfast alone had ruined the neighborhood and now this is going too far. She, well, she threatened that they wouldn't stand for it and to watch out."

Anne laid down her pen and sat back in her chair. "Whoa. I wonder what brought that on."

"They have a point," Hope said.

"What? You're supposed to be on our side," Kandi said.

"I'm not on any side. I'm just saying that we weren't very thoughtful when we decided to start this up. Remember how it was going to be something small? And now it seems to have taken on a life of its own. Between the herbal shop, visiting mom in the nursing home, and all the work at the Inn, I'm—well, I'm just going to say it. I'm burned out." Tears floated in her eyes.

"Oh, Hope. I'm so sorry." Kandi popped up from her chair and rushed over to envelop Hope in a hug.

Anne reached out to Hope. "Why haven't you said anything? I thought with the staff we'd hired, that things were better. I'm sorry, too. I've been pretty oblivious about all this, and I should have known better than to not check with the neighbors before I accepted this event. I know we have some maintenance things coming up with the Inn—new paint, possible new roof, and I think at some point, we're going to have to address the windows, which are giving us some problems too."

Hope shook her head. "It's not just that. I'm feeling out of sorts. I feel like my entire life is spent working—and for what? It's not like I'm money-driven. And now we've upset the neighbors who purchased their home years ago, envisioning a quiet cul-de-sac, not cars going in and out all the time."

Anne glanced over to Kandi, who nodded. "Yes, that's why the May family left and sold their house. Now it's been broken up into four apartments. I hate seeing these beautiful old homes changed into apartments."

Anne rose and crossed the floor. Pouring water into the kettle, she pulled out cups from the nearby cabinet. "It's not like we have control over what someone does after they buy a house."

Hope replied, "That's not really true. We started it by converting this place into a bed-and-breakfast."

"I thought we'd all agreed it was a good idea. Now

you're saying you don't think it is?" Anne asked.

Hope didn't respond. Anne grabbed a jar of Darjeeling tea, spooning it into a large muslin tea bag before turning back to Hope and Kandi. "Anyway, now we have this wedding. I don't think we can cancel at this late of a date."

"No, we can't. I...well, I'm having second thoughts about the whole wedding event thing. It's a lot more work, especially on Kandi doing all the food. And it's also a lot more risk. We've already committed to this one, but I want us to rethink hosting anything like this in the future."

Kandi's ponytail bounced as she clapped her hands, always exhibiting an exuberance and joy even now in her twenties. "I'm, like, *so* excited. I've been reading the papers—"

"You mean the gossip rags—" Anne said. She also noted Kandi's habit of slipping in the extra word whenever she became excited. At least it wasn't as much as it had been when they first met. Though sometimes, the likes in her speech seemed to take on a life of their own.

"Whatever. Anyway, from what I've read, Rayne Phillips from *Denver News* met her fiancé through a charity event they were covering. His family is from the UK, so he's English—"

"You mean British?"

Kandi knit her brows together. "What?"

"Never mind. I think it's all to do with where they live. But don't quote me on that. I'm not an expert on it." Anne busied herself with setting the cups on the table.

"Anyway, he's got one of those fancy names. Let me see if I remember." Kandi tapped her chin with her finger. "Oh, yeah. Richard Albert Lawrence Redmond-Burley. Fancy, right?"

Hope sighed. "What difference does it make to us? We've committed to doing this wedding, but after it's over, let's have a sit-down to discuss how we want to move forward and about this place."

Anne set the sugar bowl, along with a jar of honey and the teapot with the tea steeping, on the table. "Technically, this is still yours, Hope. I'd say it's up to you what you do with the house. It's your inheritance."

"I'm aware, but I also know we agreed to start it, and I want us all to come together—"

"Oh, no. Are you thinking about shutting it down?" Kandi pulled out a pitcher of milk from the fridge and went back to her seat.

"I'm not sure. But for now, let's focus on this event. Okay?" Hope responded.

"Agreed. From what I understand, the wedding party is going to be tiny. Intimate is how Rayne Phillips described it. So, we'll only have to include about fifty chairs. The evening before, we'll host the rehearsal dinner. How's that coming along, Kandi?" Anne asked.

"Good. I've spoken to Rayne's assistant, Ivy, who gave me a list of approved items and a longer list of items that are off limits. Geez, these people are so picky. And get this. She wants ten courses. Primarily for photos is what I'm guessing."

"Good grief. Are you sure you can manage that?" Anne removed the tea bag from the pot before pouring the fragrant tea into the cups.

Kandi popped up and went over to the countertop, where a covered dish held an assortment of tiny desserts. "Here, you can be my guinea pigs for these."

Hope took one from the offered tray. "They look lovely." She took a bite, "Oh, wow. Yummy, too." She set it on the small plate Anne placed in front of her and added some milk to her cup.

"It's lemon curd cake. I tried to combine some American and English foods."

Anne popped the entire petit four in her mouth, cooing over the tart lemon and the sweetness of the white cake.

"So, is there anything we can do to help with the food or the service that evening?"

Kandi shook her head. "Nope. I've roped Stewart and Molly into being servers, along with some of their friends from college. I'll have them dressed in black pants, crisp white shirts, and brocade vests under jackets."

Anne picked up her cup before replying. "That seems like a lot with the vests."

"It's because of the photos. It sounds like they're wanting to ensure good photography shots. They're paying for the jackets and the vests."

"All show. Remember when newscasters were journalists first? Now they're all celebrities spouting off opinions, and you can barely tell them apart. Look at the two women from their station—both with long blonde hair, makeup that must take an hour to apply, and they all wear these tight-fitting, spandex-looking dresses in solid colors. Barbie doll broadcasters," Hope said.

Anne set her cup down as she laughed at Hope, who ran her fingers through her cropped brown hair and face free of any makeup. In others, Anne would have thought Hope was showing jealousy, but she knew Hope to be a confident woman who couldn't care less about other opinions. Anne admired Hope, who had been the sole care-giver of her elderly mother until her mother's habits of escaping their home had forced Hope to place her in a protective environment. She also ran Carolan Springs local herbal shoppe and, as a licensed physician, had a thriving practice for locals. Maybe Hope was simply going through that time in middle-age when you started questioning your life and wondering what the future held.

After having been jolted from her seemingly perfect life, Anne's move to Carolan Springs had been perfect for healing. A divorce, a total lifestyle overhaul, friends who had become family members, and now, her engagement to Carson. She fiddled with the ring on her finger, lost in her thoughts.

"Anne, did you hear me?" Hope asked.

"What? Oh, sorry. I was in my own little world for

a while."

While Anne was in her thoughts, Hope had retrieved a spreadsheet printout which now sat in front of her on the table.

"I said that they've reserved the Inn for an entire week. Their production people will show up first, and they'll be staying over in your upstairs apartment." Anne had finally finished the third-floor rooms, similar to the attic apartment in the Brandywine Inn, though she had divided it up into a few separate bedrooms for those who wanted a bit of privacy from their companions. It was a self-contained apartment that could be rented out and was accessed through a back entrance, so there was no need to enter her part of the home. It would come in handy for people vacationing in Colorado in the summer and for holiday tourists, bringing in some extra funds which would help with the old Victorian's upkeep.

"Got it. I've already heard from them—they'll be arriving in a few days."

Hope looked back at her spreadsheet. "The primary guests will start arriving on Thursday, though most will come up on Friday. This includes the bride and groom and the maid-of honor, Casey Hudson."

"The other newscaster?"

"Yes," Hope responded.

"They look like they could be sisters. Both same height and frame with that long blonde hair." Kandi pulled up a picture of them on her phone.

Hope and Anne glanced at the picture of the two

statuesque women in similar bandage-style dresses, white, perfect teeth smiling at the camera. The graphic underneath noted, "Award-winning team at WFGH of Rayne Phillips and Casey Hudson."

"Let me see that." Anne reached for Kandi's phone before making the picture larger. She laughed. "Look at this guy in the back. He doesn't look too happy." She turned the phone around so Hope and Kandi could see the photo. Just barely in the camera range, a portly man with a rumpled olive shirt and scruffy beard scowled toward the pair.

"Oh, that's the cameraman. He came out here a few days ago, checking location spots and asking about lighting."

Anne held the phone so Hope could see the picture.

"Well, whoever he is, he doesn't look thrilled at the pair in that picture. Probably tired of doing all the heavy lifting—literally—while the people on-screen get all the credit."

Anne handed Kandi her phone back before standing up. "Whew, that tea went right through me. I'm off to the bathroom. Back in a jiff."

Kandi, lost on scrolling through her phone, didn't say anything as Hope nodded and went back to work on the spreadsheet, ensuring nothing fell through the cracks. Anne walked out of the kitchen and into the back office. "Kandi!"

Kandi and Hope appeared in the doorway to the bathroom.

Anne sighed. "Can you explain to me why there are ducklings in the bathtub?"

Hope bent down and ran a finger over a duck's back. "Oh, they're darling."

"Darling or no, what are they doing here?" Anne asked.

Kandi shrugged. "I needed to put them somewhere where I could take them in and out on nice days. Duck eggs are wonderful and rich for baking, but I can't put them in with my chickens. They're already so territorial. It's not like we use this tub, so I brought them here. I can still get my work done and check on them through the day."

"I can't believe you. What am I saying—of course, I'm not surprised. But this is our bathroom."

"If you're afraid they're going to watch you, you could pull the shower curtain."

"Um, no, I'm not worried about ducks that tiny paying any attention to me, but won't they fly out? And we don't even have a shower curtain in here since we don't use this tub." The old cook's quarters had been converted to the Inn's office and a bathroom installed in a smaller room, for their personal use.

"No, they won't. And I put down rubber mats so I can keep the tub clean, and they won't slip. But it's nice and warm in here for them."

Anne shook her head. "I never know what to expect with you, but I guess it keeps me on my toes. Now you all go on out of here so I can have some privacy. Or what there is of it."

9

Hope and Kandi left the bathroom, and Anne closed the door behind them. A duck looked up at her. "Don't be looking at me, or I'll make sure your name is L'Orange."

The rest of the day passed fairly quickly as the team went over the rest of the preparations for the upcoming events. Hope supervised the housekeeping staff while Anne spent her time arranging flowers for the guest rooms. She wrapped peony buds in the newspaper, stashing them on a refrigerator shelf next to others she'd done earlier. These would adorn the tables for the rehearsal dinner. She'd tried to find bluebells to incorporate the English theme, but they wouldn't have lasted, so she'd scrapped the idea.

That night, she arrived home tired and ready to soak in a hot bath before vegging on some mindless television before bed. The phone rang just as she had shucked into some leggings and an oversized pajama top. It was Carson.

"Hello, you," Anne said.

"Hello you too. Good day?"

"Yes, pretty much all caught up with the main items for the wedding events."

"Listen, after this is over, how about you and I go off somewhere? Spend a month or two traveling."

"What do you mean?" Anne asked.

"I mean what are we waiting for? Let's get married

and start our life together. Neither of us care about a big wedding. Let's have a honeymoon that kicks off our retirement."

Anne adjusted the phone. "Retirement. What are you talking about?"

"I shouldn't have broached it over the phone. The election for sheriff is coming up again. I'm thinking of supporting and endorsing Ruiz for the position."

"But you love your work."

"I did. But I'm tired of it. I don't want to waste my good years working. I want to spend more time with you. Let's figure out what we want to do—together."

Anne fell silent.

"Anne?"

"Yes, I'm here. I just, well, this is sudden. I need some time to think about it. I have the Inn and my gardening consulting is growing."

"I'm not saying you can't do that. I'm just saying, let's take some time to figure out what we both want."

"Sure. Of course."

"Why do I hear a 'but' in there?" Carson asked.

"You don't. I'm tired, that's all. My brain's not firing on all cylinders. Can we talk about this when you come over for dinner tomorrow?"

"Of course. Sweet dreams. I love you."

"I love you too."

"Do you?"

"What kind of question is that?"

"Just wondering, that's all."

"Well, stop your wondering. You know I love you.

We seem to keep having this same argument." She pulled her legs up to her chest.

"No arguments. But we have decisions to make on what the rest of our lives looks like. And it's always put on the back burner. For later."

Anne didn't know what to say.

"See you tomorrow," he said.

The line went dead, and Anne stared at the phone. Her cold feet about getting married for a second time continued to cause friction between the pair. She knew Carson was nothing like her first husband, but being in charge of her own life now was something she didn't want to give up. Would her need for control cause her to lose out on his love? He certainly wouldn't wait on her forever.

She reached for the remote control and flipped through the channels. Casey Hudson was filling in for Rayne Phillips, though you could barely tell the pair apart. She was effortless in her delivery of the day's news, signing off with her trademark line, "I'm Casey Hudson, bringing you news you can use."

Anne clicked off the television and plodded upstairs to bed where a black ball of fur took center place on her pillow.

"Mouser, you do not get to hog my pillow." She picked up the cat, who responded with a grievous meow at being displaced. Anne punched her pillow and flipped it to the cooler side before turning off the light. She lay in the dark, her mind a blank. As her eyes closed in sleep, she dreamed of television cameras, tables stacked with cakes made of lemon curd, and her running in slow motion, her feet encased in towering stilettoes, her hair covered by a blond wig. A cameraman followed behind with others, yelling out, "What's your plans for your life?"

Chapter Two

Sunlight spilled through the window, announcing the new day. Anne moaned and rolled away from the brightness, pulling the covers over her head. She'd had a fitful night, coming in and out of dreams, waking up, and struggling to fall back to sleep.

Anne yawned loudly, causing Mouser to jump up from his spot and pad off the bed until his paws hit the floor. Thank heavens for the automatic feeders, so she didn't have to get up right away, though she couldn't stay in bed too long, as she had a full day ahead of her. She turned over on her back, pulling the covers down before raising her arms and stretching. Another loud yawn escaped. She would need some good, strong coffee this morning after that restless night.

The thought came unbidden: *What if you didn't have to do or go anywhere? What if you could choose what and when and how you spent your days?* She pictured herself waking up next to Carson, able to spend their days however they chose.

"So, why are you dragging your feet, then?"

Her question lingered in the air with no answer returned. Why *was* she dragging her feet on moving forward with a man she loved?

Anne glanced over to the clock. Seven-thirty. She didn't have to be over to the Inn until later. She knew Kandi would already be busy in the kitchen there, as she was one of those crazy early bird people who loved rising with the crack of dawn. A thought came to her. She could create a bouquet for the Coles and include a plate of Kandi's confections as well. Maybe Hope was right, and they hadn't been good neighbors. She could at least attempt to make amends.

After she'd dressed in jeans and a chambray shirt, she made her way downstairs to where Mouser sat licking his paw. He'd eaten his earlier treats and was now ready for the main course. He meowed as she came into the kitchen.

"Yes, master. I am getting your food right now." She popped open a small can and set it in his bowl before taking it over to his preferred spot in the kitchen. A deep purring sounded in the room as he tucked into his feast of fishy delight. Anne pulled a straw hat from the rack and shucked her feet into slides before making her way over to the Inn. The day was warm, and birds trilled their songs from within the branches of the lilac hedge.

Anne entered the kitchen to find Kandi singing along to music only she could hear in her earbuds. She grinned as she saw Anne and pointed to the coffeepot.

"Ahh, you know me." Anne poured a cup of the hot, dark brew, adding in some cream before pointing to Kandi's ear.

"Hiya. What's up?"

Anne explained her plan to Kandi.

"That's, like, a great idea. I have some fresh blueberry and lemon scones I can send as well. Let me make up a gift basket while you're doing the flowers."

"Great. If you need me, I'll be in the dining room." While they prepared for the upcoming event, Anne had garnished the dining room for her prep work since she knew Kandi would require the entire kitchen. The dining chairs had been moved into the other room, and the table was covered with plastic and newspaper. Various vases sat on the sideboard, awaiting the arrangements from the coolers.

Anne got busy creating an arrangement of ranunculus, dahlias, and snapdragons. She finished it with some bright yellow daffodils. Then she went in to where Kandi had created a lovely basket of goodies for the couple. "Oh, that's lovely. I'm sure we'll be able to win them over with those goodies and the flowers."

"I wouldn't be so sure. Mrs. Cole was pretty upset when she found out about the wedding events. She said it was the last straw."

"You don't think she'd cause any issues, do you?"

Kandi shrugged. "Who knows? When people get upset, there's no telling what they might do. Though she's always been nice before. I've never seen her so upset."

"Well, we can at least try. Let me wash my hands, and then I'll take these items over to her."

"Oh, good. I don't want to be in the line of fire again."

"When I get back, I'll work on putting the dining room back properly before everyone arrives, so they'll be able to use the space."

"Ah, yes. Good point," Kandi answered.

Anne made her way to the bathroom, where she washed her hands and spent a few minutes enjoying the ducks, who were nibbling on some herbs from the gardens. Back in the kitchen, she picked up the basket and mouthed, "Wish me luck" to Kandi, who replied by making a goofy face. Anne chuckled and shook her head before retrieving the flowers. She made her way across the street and noticed some painters working on the Coles' curb, painting it white. She said hello and made her way up to the door. Transferring the vase to her other hand, she rang the bell.

Mrs. Cole, a stout woman with a dour expression, answered. Her gray hair was clipped short and beady eyes stared at Anne. From what Anne had heard from Kandi, Mrs. Cole had been a teacher in her youth, and she would have been able to stop any commotion with that look. "Yeah, what can I do for you?"

Anne forced herself to smile. "Mrs. Cole, we wanted to give you and Mr. Cole a basket of goodies and some flowers from us and the Brandywine Inn."

"You ain't going to bribe me."

"What? I'm sorry—"

"Code enforcement. I called them on you all." She pointed with a bony finger toward the Inn. "Disgraceful. Ruining our neighborhood. Coming in here, changing everything without so much as a—well, it doesn't matter. That place needs shutting down."

"Mrs. Cole. I assure you that we got all the permits—"

"I don't care what you have to say. You don't have events registration and parking."

A noise caught Anne's attention. A young man in biker's clothes—shoes, hat and gloves—was toting an expensive bike out onto the porch next door.

"See what I mean? You did this!" She pointed at Anne.

Flustered and almost at her breaking point, Anne knew she had to get away before she did or said something she'd regret. "I wanted to bring this over to you."

The woman stood with her arms folded, unmoving.

Anne spied a table next to a glider on the porch. "I'll just set it here." She placed the basket on the table before turning back to see the woman had already shut her front door. So much for goodwill.

As Anne made her way back to the Inn, she glanced to what the men were painting onto the curb. No Parking. Great. That would mean extra hauling of items or figuring out parking in each of the drives.

She returned to the Inn and told Kandi about the encounter with Mrs. Cole.

"I told you. She's so mean. I didn't have her in high school, but everyone who got her tried as hard as they could to get in a different class. I bet she'll take the goodies, though. She has a sweet tooth. And I've taken her things before during the holidays or when they've been sick."

"Who knows? But I did my part. You have any

more coffee left?"

"Yep. I just made a new pot," Kandi said.

Anne refilled her cup from earlier and made her way to the dining room. She pulled back the lacy curtains and, sure enough, the flowers and basket were no longer on the table outside. Anne picked at her cuticles. If Mrs. Cole complained to the code enforcement office, that could cause some big problems for them. She hadn't thought about events needing a different permit. Mrs. Cole was definitely serious if she'd have no parking painted on her curb. What else was the woman willing to do to hinder the event going forward?

Anne dressed in a mint sheath to welcome the wedding party and production crew. Hope and Kandi were already at the Inn, working on trays of canapes and other light refreshments. Today would be about finalizing everything before the rehearsal dinner tomorrow. Anne and Hope had made it out onto the front porch when an expensive Mercedes pulled up.

A gentleman appeared from the driver's side. He was tall and well-built, with a chiseled jaw and head full of jet black hair. His posture was erect, and he bore the signs of wealth like someone else wore clothing. Surveying the area, he closed his door before coming around and opening the door for the woman in the passenger seat. Rayne Phillips emerged from the vehicle dressed in an expensive white pants suit. She reached out to take the man's hand, and her substantial engagement ring caught the light. Anne waited as the man shut the door behind her, and they advanced up the sidewalk.

Anne spoke first, extending her hand. "Hello, I'm Anne Freemont. Welcome to Brandywine Inn."

The handsome gentleman responded, "Very good to meet you. My name is Richard Redmond-Burley."

Rayne spoke up. "Ral, I left my purse in the car. Would you be a dear and fetch it for me?"

"Certainly, love." He nodded to Anne before making his way back to the car.

"I wanted to have him out of earshot for a bit. He doesn't need to be bothered with all the ins and outs of this. If we could have one of your people take care of him, that will be helpful."

One of our people? Anne shot Hope a quick glance. They'd dealt with persnickety patrons before, and this looked to be no different. Having worked with the assistant, things would be much easier if she continued handling things now.

Hope responded, "We have prepared some light hors d'oeurves and drinks inside. Once the rest of your group arrive, we can go over everything for tomorrow and the following days if that works for you."

"Fine. Has Casey Hudson arrived yet?" She glanced toward the door.

"No, not yet."

"Not surprising. She's always up to something to

cause me angst. Oh, well. Shall we?"

"Hope, can you escort Ms. Phillips inside, please?"

Kandi had joined them unbeknownst to Anne, and she bobbed with excitement. "I can do it!"

"Wonderful. If you'll follow Kandi, she'll escort you upstairs. Do you have any bags that need to be brought in?"

"We do. Ral can take care of them for me. Ral, you coming?"

"On my way, dearest."

He made his way to her side, wrapping his arm around her waist in a protective mode for a brief moment before following behind holding the bags.

"This way." Kandi held the door open for Rayne.

After Kandi took the pair inside, Hope whispered, "What have you gotten us into this time?"

Anne replied, "A lot of money to replace the furnace with a new, efficient model and free publicity for the Inn."

"Yes, but at what cost?"

Anne shrugged. "Probably our sanity."

"Well, at least you're honest there. Plus, all that PDA feels like a show. Wonder how long that's going to last?"

Anne didn't have time to respond as they turned at the sound of other vehicles arriving. One was a gray sedan holding Casey Hudson, the cameraman, Lee Branson, and another woman. The vehicle that followed them was a white Sprinter van driven by a male. As the others got out of their vehicles and approached the house, the driver went around to the back of the van and climbed inside.

Casey strode confidently toward the pair. "Hello! I'm Casey Hudson. You must be Anne, and you're Hope." She held out her hand. Unlike the snootiness they'd felt from Rayne, Kasey appeared to be more down-to-earth in her approach to others. "This is Lee. I think you may have already met. He'll be doing most of the camera work. The other gentleman, Scott, will also be doing camera work, and there should be a photographer also arriving tomorrow. Oh, and this is Jodie Miller. She's our producer. She won't be here tomorrow but will be here on Saturday."

After they finished introductions, another van pulled up with a dress shop logo on the side. Anne watched as two individuals went around to the back of the van, pulling out garment bags. "Ah, here's the wedding attire for the next few days."

The two ladies walked over to the steps, where Hope stepped forward to greet them.

"I'll take them up to the rooms," she said. After she'd ushered the group up the steps, they followed Hope inside. As Anne allowed everyone to go in, she turned to see Mrs. Cole on her porch, arms crossed against her chest, a scowl on her face. Not knowing what else to do, Anne waved at the woman, who turned and disappeared back into her house.

Great. A diva in the house and an adversary on the outside.

The ladies from the dress shop made their way down the stairs, having deposited the bags of clothing upstairs. They spoke with Rayne and Ral, who had moved into the living area where Kandi had set trays of refreshments on a mahogany pie crust table. In the corner, a glass-topped trolley held buckets of ice with drinks in them, along with tall glasses and an assortment of water and soda. Kandi had outdone herself on making everything look perfect for when they arrived. The others had joined Rayne as well. Beside Ral, Lee had grabbed a soda and was sitting in a chair, fiddling with his camera. Candace's voice was intent as she spoke to Rayne and Casey about some notes she held in her hand. As Anne studied the group, she realized that Rayne was shorter than Casey by at least a few inches. Casey wore ballet flats while Rayne had on a pair of stacked sandals.

A male voice startled her. Lee must have moved while she'd been watching the women. For a large man, he moved quietly from one place to the other. "I said, hard to tell them apart, huh?"

Anne turned toward the cameraman. "Um, yes, they look so much alike."

"They really don't. It's the makeup, hair color and style, and of course, clothing. Away from the studio, they get to enjoy being a bit different."

"What's the purpose of them looking so much alike? You'd think that they'd want to look different for the camera."

He shook his head. "Nope. You have to realize that

television news is a bit like grabbing a burger from a fast-food joint. You go there because it's always the same. You want the same thing every time. So, when one person is off, you still get the same. You know they're different, but subconsciously, your mind is calmed. Same clothing, hair, look."

"Ah, I always wondered about it. Those same clothes, normally red or blue, with three-quarter sleeves. Makes more sense now."

"Yes. And the wavy, blonde hair as well. But trust me, they're not the same. Especially where it counts. One is an angel, and one is a devil." He winked and walked away, leaving Anne's mouth gaping.

If what he'd said were true, which was which? And why would he even say such a thing? She turned back to the party. Hope was showing Rayne the seating chart for the dinner, but it was the look on one person's face that grabbed her attention.

Love.

It was written all over Ral's face, but his gaze didn't rest on Rayne, it rested on Casey.

Chapter Three

Cars started arriving early the next morning. Rayne had arrived with her assistant, who must be the Ivy Kandi had referred to during their conversation. Ivy looked to be in her late teens or early twenties. Compared to the highly made-up persona of her employer, Ivy was a mousey woman who trailed behind Rayne with a clipboard.

Anne stood outside, directing vehicles to park in her driveway or in Kandi's if they weren't unloading. She couldn't figure out why they needed so many things for a small wedding. Thankfully, it was only a couple of days, and the crew would be gone.

A voice called out. It was Rayne's assistant. Anne faced her.

"Oh, sorry, you startled me. There seems like a lot of stuff coming and going for their wedding."

"Especially after the fact," Ivy said.

"After the fact?" Anne asked.

The woman sighed, tapping her palm to her forehead. "Ugh, I have to learn to keep my mouth shut."

Anne laughed. "No worries. That would make two of us. Don't worry. I keep secrets. But if it can help us, I'd really like to know so we can ensure that everything runs smoothly. I'm Anne, by the way."

The woman took Anne's offered hand. "Ivy. Since

I've already let some of it out of the bag, I might as well finish it. The fact is Rayne and Richard are already married. They did it when they were on vacation in the Bahamas. This is for one thing and one thing only."

It came to Anne immediately. Money. They needed pictures of the couple exchanging vows, having the fancy reception so they could sell the photos to the media. No wonder Rayne had requested ten courses. It's not that she wanted them so much as she wanted to be known as having them.

Anne couldn't help herself as curiosity took over. "How much are we talking?"

"Hundreds of thousands. Then there are the designers for the clothing, the jewelry, etc."

Anne waved to the Inn. "Why our little spot?"

"Rayne had me pick somewhere outside of Denver. Not too far. She said that the chances of things being leaked are less out here, but it's close enough to get back for evening shows."

"Will she still be going on television tonight?"

Ivy shook her head. "No, but Casey will front the 10 pm news with the co-host, Brandon Sanders."

A large van pulled up just as two men exited the house next door to the Coles. One was the biker Anne had seen the other day, and one was dressed in a priest's dark black robe. Her attention returned to the media van. "What's this doing here?"

"It's a mini-studio. For editing or doing on-site shows. Not sure why it's here, but Rayne must have requested it." She leafed through the paperwork on her clipboard. "Hmm. I don't see it on here. I need to go find out. Will you excuse me?"

"Sure." Anne watched as Ivy trudged back to the house. Hard to believe she was Rayne's assistant. It didn't seem like they would gel very well, but that probably wasn't the most important thing, anyway. Anne turned back to see men putting up a large green screen, effectively removing the cars parked in Kandi's driveway and her house. Others rushed past her to the back yard carrying similar looking items.

A horn sounded. Rayne had returned.

Today she was outfitted in a blue sheath dress with sky-high tan heels which lengthened her legs. A man dressed in a suit hurried over and opened her door while three photographers snapped shots of her exiting the car, waving, and walking down the sidewalk. While most women pushed their hair away from their face, Anne noticed that the newscaster parted her hair in the back, so she had a full head of flowing waves framing her face for photos.

Tricks of the trade, Anne supposed. Since the focus was on your face, pulling your hair forward achieved even more volume.

After a few moments, Rayne held up her hand in a motion to stop before returning to the car and repeating the process again. Anne couldn't believe the filming production to get a few clips or stills of Rayne's arrival. Another car arrived and Richard exited it. He was wearing a tailored suit with a tie that coordinated with Rayne's dress. The process repeated with him and then with the couple. More photographers had arrived, and they gathered in front of the pair who stood in front of the green screen. Rayne posed with the ring prominently showing as she held his arm.

I wonder what they'll show as the backdrop, Anne thought. Maybe picturesque snow-capped mountains.

After a break during which the newer photographers left, Rayne stepped over to where Anne stood. "Hello, again. We came a bit early to get in some pictures. I hope that's all right with you."

"Of course. Can I show you to your rooms?"

Rayne shook her head. "I'm going to be in the news van working. Ral?"

He brushed her hair with his lips. "As long as I have a quiet place to make some phone calls, I'll be fine."

"I can show you upstairs where it should be quiet," Anne interjected.

"Brilliant." He gestured for her to lead the way.

They went up to the second floor, where Ivy stood with a bag that most likely contained one of Rayne's dresses. "If you'll follow me up another flight, we have a small apartment that I believe will suit your needs."

He smiled. "Lead on."

Anne unlocked the door at the top and went over to open the curtains. "There's a kettle here for tea, or if you prefer coffee, we can send some up. The refrigerator is stocked with regular and sparkling water and some juices and sodas. And this basket has some treats if you get hungry. If you need anything, you can call down to the office, and Hope will answer."

"Thank you so much. This should work well for my needs."

Anne held on to the doorknob. "If you don't mind me asking, how did you and Rayne meet?"

"Not at all. It was a charity event. They were invited as guests and covering it for the news."

"They?"

"Yes, Rayne and Casey Hudson."

Anne smiled at him, "They look a lot alike, don't they?"

"For the camera. But they're very different people." His expression dropped.

"Sorry, I didn't mean to pry."

He shook his head. "Sometimes, we see what we want to see. I thought I knew someone, and it turned out that they were not what I thought." He smiled. "But life goes on, and good things are on the horizon."

"Yes, that's true. Congratulations."

"Thank you. Now I must attend to this phone call."

"Of course. Again, let us know if you need anything else." She closed the door and made her way down the stairs. Something had happened. Was it something between him and Casey? Had Casey rejected his advances? He had looks, a pedigree, wealth, and was noted as one of the most eligible bachelors in Denver. He may not have meant to reveal his feelings, but there was no use denying the look on

31

his face when he'd spotted Casey. So, why was he marrying Rayne?

As Anne reached the next floor, she thought she'd check in on Ivy. They'd devoted one room to being Rayne's dressing room, so Ivy must be working with the gowns. The door was open, but Anne rapped on the frame before entering. "Hello, Ivy?"

Ivy turned around, her face flushed. "Oh, Anne. What is it?"

"Just checking to see if you need anything."

"Oh, thanks." Ivy set down a pair of scissors and picked up the dress from the bed. She walked over and hung it on a hook on the closet door.

"That dress is beautiful." Anne admired the detailing around the bodice and the beautiful satin skirt. Lace inserts along the waist, sleeves, and the bottom of the skirt were nice touches.

"Yes, she has three, along with tonight's dress. One for the dinner tonight, one for the ceremony, one for the reception, and her outfit for when they leave."

"Are they taking another honeymoon?"

Ivy shook her head. "I think they're going over to England for a while."

Anne responded, "No family attending tomorrow?"

"No. His parents died when he was young, and he spent most of his formative years in boarding school."

"Oh, that's terrible. I can't imagine growing up without my parents. What about Rayne's?"

"She doesn't speak about them, so not sure if

they're estranged or if they too passed away earlier. Listen, I need to finish this. Anything else I can do for you?"

Anne laughed. "No, I'm the one who needs to ask you that."

"I'm fine. Everything is under control," she replied.

"Okay, well, I'll leave you to it then."

Anne made her way downstairs, where every space seemed to be filled with people standing around, chatting with one another. Some were in jeans and polo shirts, while others were dressed in more formal attire. It was a strange mix of people. She pushed past a group standing in the hall and made her way back to the kitchen, where Kandi was putting on the finishing touches for the evening's meal. She waved a hand to Anne as she continued piping dots on clear plates. Hope was typing in the computer when Anne entered the office and plopped down on the chair in front of the desk.

"What do you think?" Hope questioned.

"I don't know what to think. This is the strangest thing I think I've ever encountered."

"Do tell."

"Well, first of all, everything is fake. They put up green screens out front, and when I peeked out an upper-story window coming downstairs, I see they've put up another one behind where the bride and groom are sitting. Ivy told me they're already married, and I'd swear that Ral is in love with Casey."

VIKKI WALTON

"That is something. Well, I'll add this to your day. I got a call from Mrs. Cole, who's on the warpath again with all the comings and goings. She threatened to call the cops for us disturbing the peace."

"I wish I would have thought to pay for a hotel for them for the next few days," Anne replied.

Hope tilted the chair back. "We have to take her concerns seriously. This isn't Main Street, but we've turned it into our own little show. And with the current goings-on, no wonder she's upset. It's like a theatrical production going on here. What happened to 'it will be a small wedding party and dinner' that we agreed to with them?"

Anne sighed. "Yes, I agree that it's not what we thought. I don't know what to do at this juncture. They may have taken advantage of us, but we won't let it happen again next time."

"That's what I'm saying, Anne. There can be no 'next time' here."

"So, no more events? What about all the money we spent on the gazebo, and—"

Hope sighed. "I don't want to talk about this right now. Let's get through this, um, craziness, and then we can all sit down afterward and figure it out. I know Kandi loves all this, but even she's been a bit overwhelmed with all the changes to the menu and so many rules to follow. She loves cooking, but she's not a caterer with a large staff. It's a lot of pressure on her to get this right."

"I'll go see what I can do to help her." Anne stood.

"Hope?"

"Yes?"

"Thank you."

"For what?"

"For being a voice of reason and keeping us grounded. I know that I sometimes can get carried away with ideas. I'm glad you're my friend."

"You too. Now I have to get back to adding up these numbers. I want to keep ahead of things to ensure we attain the expected profit from this venture."

"Okay, I'm just going to hit the bathroom and get back out front to direct traffic." Anne opened the door to the bathroom. Stepping inside, she glanced over to the tub. No ducks. She yelled out to Hope, "Did Kandi move the ducks?"

"No, why?"

Anne came to the door. "They're not here."

"What?" Hope rose from her chair. "Let's ask Kandi."

They went into the kitchen, where Kandi was sliding a tray of plates into rented coolers. "Look, this is my amuse-bouche for the start of the meal."

"Wonderful. Listen, I'm here to help with whatever you need but wanted to ask what you did with the ducks."

"The ducks?" Kandi's face fell. "Was I supposed to have duck on the menu?" She raced over to the desk, outlining the menu.

"No, we're wondering about the ducklings in the

bathtub. Where are they?"

"I don't know. I didn't move them!"

"Who could have taken them, and why?" Anne took Hope's arm. "Have you been in the office all this morning?"

Hope shook her head. "No, I was helping people set up computers or taking them over to your upstairs apartment. The doors are open, so anyone could have come in and taken them."

"But why would they do such a thing?"

"Oh, no." Anne raced out to the back yard and over to the gazebo. Flowers she had planted were trampled or missing their buds while the ducklings played in a mud puddle created by a hose left on. Some had walked on the path leading to the gazebo, and a path of muddy web prints marked the carpet. "Who could have—" Immediately, she knew who had let the ducklings out of the tub and created the havoc in the back yard. "Shoot. No one was watching the back. I bet Mrs. Cole did this."

"I doubt that. Whoever did it, we have to get it cleaned up before—"

"What's going on out here?" It was Rayne.

"Just a little mishap. That's all. We'll have it fixed in no time." Anne grabbed one duckling before it took a bite of another plant.

"Maybe it's a sign."

"What?"

"Ghosts. I've heard there have been deaths at this place. Maybe they're trying to wreck my wedding!"

Rayne cried out.

"Don't be silly, there's no such thing—" Anne stopped when Hope shot her a look to be quiet.

Hope moved forward. "Not to worry. We'll have this cleaned up in a jiff. These just escaped from the house next door. We'll get them locked up securely. Kandi, why don't you show Ms. Phillips the wonderful amuse-bouches for tonight?"

Kandi got the hint and scurried over to take Rayne inside. Grabbing a cardboard box from the back porch, Anne spied Casey watching from the driveway. Had she seen the entire encounter, or worse yet, had she instigated it? So many people had come and gone during the day it was hard to know who could have even known about the ducks. It could have been anyone in the house .

They rounded up the ducklings and hosed down the footprints left behind. Anne would need to do some fill of the flowers that were damaged, but most looked fine. She could take some from her own yard if needed. After putting the ducklings back in the bathroom, they locked the door to the office. Anne turned over traffic control to Hope while she repaired the back yard, adding in some pansies and other greenery she had left over at her house to the spaces trampled on by the ducklings. Anne checked her watch. She could go take a hot shower before the dinner started in a few hours. Thankfully, they'd waited to have it later when it would be cooler and the lighting would be on, providing a wonderful ambience for the event. Hope had left when Stewart and Molly arrived with their friends, and Kandi was busy distributing filled trays with sandwiches and crudites for the various crewmembers. She waved at them, saying she'd be back soon, and headed home.

While dressing, Anne thought back to the ducks. It made no sense. However, it wouldn't take much time to sneak into the office, find the ducks, and let them go in the back yard. With so much going on and people moving between floors, Kandi and Hope had been kept busy and so the kitchen had been empty for a while. It still made little sense, though. It was more of a distraction than anything else. The question was, distraction from what?

She arrived back at the house a half-hour before the reception dinner was to begin. The living room was full of people, and Ivy stood on the stair landing to gather everyone's attention. A van would be bringing in guests to the end of the street for the evening's event, so cameras and lighting had been set up in the front yard. One car would deliver a couple who would be photographed while the other car when back and picked up the next couple and so on. The news van had been moved to the end of the street, and barriers had been set up across the end of the cul-de-sac, ensuring that people crowded around to see what was going on down the block.

What a spectacle. Anne forced herself not to shake her head at how ridiculous and circus-like the event had become. Anne cringed at the thought of Mrs. Cole watching this from her house. She hadn't done her due diligence on what they had planned, and now it was causing them to regret accepting the contract. The only saving grace was that it was only one more day, and they'd be done and have a huge check in their bank account for all the hassle.

Footsteps came down the stairs behind Ivy, and Anne spied Ral in his fitted tuxedo. "Does anyone know where Rayne is? I can't seem to find her."

Ivy responded, "She went out back for a moment to check that everything is ready. Now, as I was saying—"

A scream shattered the momentary quiet.

Rayne ran into the room from the back. "A body. Wearing my wedding dress."

She collapsed into Ral's arms.

Chapter Four

Everyone rushed over to Rayne, who was hurried to the sofa in the living room. She was coming around, so Anne and Hope set off toward the back. They opened the back door to see the yard lit up with beautiful, soft lighting and candles set in hurricane globes dotting the long table and the paths.

"You go that way, and I'll head this way." Anne pointed at the main table, toward the back of the yard, as she made her way over to the gazebo.

Nothing.

She went up the stairs into the gazebo and looked around. Again, nothing. By this time, Hope had rejoined her, and others were now gathering on the back porch.

Hope yelled back at them, "All's well. There's nothing here."

They heard murmuring as the people moved back inside.

"What do you think's going on, Anne? First the ducklings, and now this. Do you think someone is doing this on purpose?"

"Well, as much as I considered Mrs. Cole with the ducklings, this makes no sense. I don't see anything that looks remotely like a person's body or a white wedding dress."

"Wait, what's that?" Hope went over to a bush and

reached out to gather a scrap of lace from a branch. She held it up to Anne. "Does this look familiar?"

Anne groaned. "Yes, it's the lace from Rayne's dress. Let's go up the back staircase and see if it matches."

As they entered the kitchen, they could hear voices speaking to Rayne, who kept repeating, "It's a sign." But it was the whispers they heard about deaths in the Inn and ghosts that caused them to glance at each other. Certainly, they'd never concealed the fact that people had died at the Inn, but they didn't want it to be the focus of anything either.

Anne signaled to Hope. "Come on. Let's check this out before anyone else comes up here."

As they made their way to the dressing room, Casey appeared at the top of the front stairs. "Oh, you frightened me. I didn't know anyone was up here."

Hope shoved the piece of lace into her pocket. "Just checking to see if anything was amiss up here."

"Amiss?" Casey asked.

"Ensuring that all rooms have everything needed for the evening. Just Inn upkeep," Anne answered.

"Oh, okay. My room seems fine, but you're welcome to look." She went back and unlocked her door, allowing Anne and Hope to enter. The room looked fine. The only thing out of place was the large dress bag hooked over the closet door.

"Have you been up here all this time?"

"Why do you ask?"

"Just curious. I thought you'd be down with the

rest of the crew."

"No, I had a bit more work to get done on scripting for tomorrow." Casey waved her hand to a desk holding a laptop.

"Oh, okay. Well, thanks. See you downstairs. And please let us know if there's anything we overlooked or that you need," Anne replied.

"Will do."

Casey locked the door behind her before heading down the main staircase.

"Are you thinking what I'm thinking?"

Anne nodded. "She could have easily slipped down the back stairs while we were all in the house's front. She had to have heard Ivy expounding on the steps below."

"But what about the wedding dress? She would have had to get into the dress, go out, and be outside where only Rayne saw her, then rush back through the kitchen and up the back stairs, only to change into her current outfit."

"And not look flustered."

"That too. Plus, what about the dress? No, something's not adding up."

"I agree with you. The question is what and who did Rayne see?"

"Let's go see if the dress is okay," Hope said.

They walked down to the dressing room where Rayne's dresses hung from various hangers and hooks. Anne pulled back the closet door. No dress.

Casey had returned. "Sorry, forgot to grab my

43

phone. All good?"

Anne nodded, as she didn't want to say anything in front of Casey. She shut the closet door and waited.

Casey spoke. "I took a peek out the window. It's enchanting. You've done a lovely job. I hope Rayne doesn't ruin it for you."

Before Anne could respond, Hope replied, "What do you mean?"

"It's a stunt. More publicity. Why do you think she chose this place?" She stared at them. "Sorry, no offense, but it's not exactly the Ritz. It's the deaths and possible ghosts. I mean, a haunted inn. You have to agree, it makes good copy. Sure, she'll have the wedding photos, and those'll sell okay. But add in something else, and bingo, you've got a better story."

"Like the saying, if it bleeds, it leads?"

Casey nodded. "There has to be some underlying drama. Something to make people pay attention." She sighed. "I'm so tired of all this. I'll be glad when Rayne moves on from the station."

"Moves on?" Anne asked.

"I'm going to take over her evening spot when she leaves with Ral. I've already been sitting in with Brandon Sanders, and polls show that we're the winning team. Don't say anything, though. It won't be announced for another month or so."

"But I thought Rayne loves her job at the station. Why would she step down and give it up now?"

Casey glanced over to the door, then lowered her voice. "Pregnant."

Anne thought back to what Ivy had said. So that must be the reason the couple had gotten married earlier. They could put the photos out and wouldn't even need to date them. Not that women didn't get pregnant before marriage, but the station had to maintain its squeaky clean image, most likely.

"Well, I guess after what happened, this means the dinner is off. We better go down and figure out the next steps."

Casey shook her head. "Not sure what you're referring to, but unless someone died, and even then, the dinner will go on. Photographers are here. You'll see. It will be like nothing ever happened. I'll be leaving early tomorrow to do the morning show, and then I'll see you all later in the afternoon." She walked over to the door before turning around. "You know what they say—the show must go on."

"Hope, what in the world? Do you think she's right? This has all been an act to produce more 'prime-time TV suspense' for the media?"

"Who knows? But I, for one, am getting a bit tired of it. Let's get down and see where we are with the dinner preparations."

By the time they made it downstairs, the living room had been emptied. Guests had arrived and were being escorted down the driveway and to the porte cochere, where photographers waited to snap pictures of the couples. Under an arch in the back, Ral stood next to Rayne, greeting guests like nothing had happened earlier.

A nudge at her arm had Anne looking to see Ivy by her side. "So, Rayne is okay now?"

"Yes, Ral convinced her it's only a bit of nerves and nothing to worry about. Plus, she already had everything planned, so no turning back now."

Movement in her own yard caught Anne's eye. It was the priest from across the street. He was partly concealed by a vehicle and the lilac hedge. Was he planning on doing the service and simply checking things out for tomorrow? Rayne saw him and excused herself from the group. She walked over to him, and it sounded like they were arguing. He sprinted away, and Rayne turned back, only to see Anne staring at her. A shocked look passed over her face, but she quickly regained her composure and waved. "Better now."

"Good."

Rayne joined Ral, and after the last guests arrived, she hooked her arm with Ral's and strode over to the table. Kandi had outdone herself, and each course brought praise from the guests. Finally, Molly and Stewart distributed champagne flutes, and Ral made a toast to Rayne. Casey was seated farther done from the couple, and while she half-heartedly raised it with her left hand, she emptied the glass with no further fanfare. Whether they had been an item, Kasey had feelings of some sort, and if his expression the other day was true, he had feelings for her. It was the proverbial triangle, and that never bode well for anyone.

As guests began leaving for the night, Anne helped

Molly and Stewart pick up the last of the dessert dishes and champagne flutes. Casey came up next to her as she fit another glass into a container. "See, I told you everything would work out okay." Her words were a bit slurred, and Anne wondered if all she'd been drinking that evening was champagne. "What Rayne wants, Rayne gets. She doesn't deserve Richard. Ah, well, what's the saying about all's fair in love and war? She won this battle. But maybe not the war. I better get up to bed as two in the morning is going to come quick."

"Two in the morning?"

"Yes. I have to get up and get ready for the show, and I'll need to make it to Denver for the shoot. Good night." She stumbled a bit before pulling off her shoes and walking across the ground in her bare feet.

Anne stared at the women's back as a chill went up her spine.

A man's deep voice uttered in her ear, "What are you thinking?"

She stifled a scream as she turned around to find Carson. *What is with everyone sneaking up behind me?* She rushed into his arms, tears pricking at her eyes. "Oh, Carson. I'm so glad you're here."

"What's the matter, N.D.?" he cooed as he used his pet name for her after the teen detective, Nancy Drew.

"Someone's going to die, and there's nothing I can do about it."

"No one's going to die."

"Yes, they are. I can feel it."

"Okay, then who?"

"That's the problem. I don't know."

When she awoke the next morning, Anne dreaded the day ahead of her. She heard movement above and knew that the crew were all busy getting ready for the day's festivities. After finally clearing up after everyone, Carson had left her and traveled back to his trailer. His new house would soon be completed, and that would involve more discussion on where the couple would live once they were married. It made her think over yesterday's events. If she was feeling some trepidation over tying the knot, why wouldn't Rayne feel the same way? Maybe someone had been playing a practical joke with the ducklings. Hopefully, her dress would show up today, but that was another issue altogether. And what about Casey? They were co-workers but certainly not friendly or caring for each other. There could be rivalry between the pair because of the anchor position but also because of Richard. Had Rayne stolen Richard from Casey so she decided the anchor spot was fair game? If everything Anne had heard was correct, Rayne wouldn't give up the spotlight without a fight, but wouldn't her marriage to Richard change everything? Did the station know that Rayne was already married, and that's why they were seeing how viewers reacted to Casey joining Brandon?

Anne pushed back the covers. She rubbed her

head. Last night had left her with a headache, and she'd struggled to decompress after the day. At two in the morning, she'd heard the crunch of tires on the gravel driveway and watched from her window as Casey left for the studio.

The doorbell rang.

Who could be here so early? She tied her robe around her waist and stuffed her feet in her slippers before heading downstairs. Opening the door, she found Candace, the producer, with a smile on her face. "Oh, I'm so sorry. I goofed. I forgot that this isn't where Casey's staying. She left her keycard at the station this morning, and she'll be needing it again."

"No, they're next door. But I'm not sure she's back yet. Come in. I can put on some coffee if you'd like a cup."

"Sounds great." Candace followed Anne inside. "I love these old homes. They have such wonderful character. They're like their own person."

"Yes, I fell in love with this place and moved here some years back." A shot of black movement caught her eye. "Oh, I hope you're okay with cats. Mouser will show up at the most inopportune times."

"I love cats." She followed Anne into the kitchen. Anne peeked out the window. There was Casey's car, so she must have already made it back from Denver.

After turning on the pot to heat the water, Anne measured out the scoops of coffee. She clicked on the start button before heading over to give Mouser his breakfast.

"How long have you been working at the station?" Anne asked Candace.

"About six months, or is it eight? Time flies these days. It's been busy, but I love the work."

Anne pulled out two mugs for the coffee. "To be honest, I don't really know what a producer does."

"Oh, well—" Her words were cut off by the sound of sirens. Anne and Candace rushed to the front door to see an ambulance pulling up next door.

Kandi was pointing to the crew, and Anne yelled at her. "What's going on?"

"It's Rayne."

Anne excused herself and rushed up to don a pair of jeans and a top. Candace had already gone next door, and Anne hurried through the kitchen door and up the back stairs to Rayne's room. The medics were working on the woman; her face pale as she answered their questions. Anne made it over to Kandi, who stood in the hallway.

"What happened?"

"I'm not sure. Ivy came up and said that Rayne was feeling ill. She was worried about her, so we called for help, just in case." Kandi groaned. "What if it's, like, food poisoning?"

"I doubt that's the issue. Others would be affected too. Where's Casey?"

"Casey?"

"Yes, if it's something like that, then others will be affected as well."

"She's probably asleep now. She was at the

station, so she's most likely catching a few z's."

A commotion made Anne turn to see Candace, a shocked expression on her face. She pointed to the doorway of Rayne's dressing room. Anne bolted over and stared at the woman lying on the floor, adorned in the missing wedding dress. It was Casey. Anne bent down and felt for a pulse. Nothing. "Help, we need help in here." Two of the medics rushed in and set to work.

Who does that leave? "Ivy. Where's Ivy?"

Kandi pointed to the smaller room down the hall.

Anne rapped on the door. "Ivy, are you in there?" She rattled the doorknob. Locked. "Ivy, open the door!" Anne banged on the door again before yelling, "Kandi, go downstairs and get the keys. Ivy, wake up!"

Anne heard voices as a stretcher came up the stairs, and they fastened an unconscious Casey to it. She rushed over to grab the keys from a breathless Kandi. She yelled to the medics. "Wait, there may be another person who needs help."

Anne fumbled with the keys, and finally, the door unlocked. But it had all been for nothing.

The room was empty.

Chapter Five

Rayne appeared at her door, clutching at her stomach. "Is she...is Casey dead?"

"No, I think we made it in time. But right now, we need to get her to the hospital."

Rayne rushed over and threw herself on the woman. "Oh, Casey, Casey!" She fought against the men who forced her hands off the woman.

As they moved down the stairs with Casey, Rayne made her way to a shocked Anne and Kandi. "Don't you see what this means? He tried to kill me!"

"What are you talking about? Let's go in and sit down. This has been a big shock for everyone."

Kandi wrung her hands. "You sure you don't want to, like, go and be checked out?"

Rayne hung her head in her hands. "No. The medics said I'm fine. I probably got rid of anything when I got sick. But don't you see, it was meant for me. Look!"

She pointed to the floor where a crumpled paper lay. Kandi reached down and opened it up. The writing was in a strong hand. *My darling, Love R.*

"That wasn't here before. I've never seen it," Rayne said. "Casey must have been holding it in her hand when they found her. She must have drunk what was meant for me." She went to reach for the glass, but Anne grabbed her wrist.

"If that's true, then this could be a crime scene, and we've already disturbed everything. Let's move downstairs to the dining room, and I'll lock these rooms until the sheriff's office can come over."

"Whatever you say." Rayne allowed Kandi to help her down the stairs while Anne locked the door.

Why had Casey been wearing Rayne's missing wedding dress? Had Casey been the one behind the theft of the dress? She made to pull her phone from her pocket but remembered she'd rushed over without grabbing it. She'd have to use the office phone. Anne went down the back stairs and opened up the office, where she made a call to Carson. He'd be there shortly and would call Deputy Ruiz, as well.

She set to work making a fresh, strong pot of coffee before taking it into the dining room where Kandi and Rayne sat. Some of the color was returning to Rayne's face, and she accepted the cup of coffee but didn't drink any of it. Rayne stared off into the distance, mixed emotions playing on her face.

"Are you sure you wouldn't like some dry toast or some tea?" Kandi asked Rayne.

"Oh, yes, not sure what I was thinking. Let Kandi make you something to settle your stomach." Anne nodded to Kandi, who looked grateful to be allowed to leave the room.

Finally, Rayne spoke. "I should have known. I've seen the way he looks at her. I'm not a fool. But I thought that once we were married, things would change. Now I realize how wrong I was. How stupid am I?" She bent over and pressed her face into her bent arms that rested on the table, her shoulders heaving with silent sobs.

"I'm sure everything will be worked out soon," Anne replied.

"Will it? I shouldn't have listened to him. Why did I—"

Kandi stopped any further conversation by carrying in a tray with toast and a pot of herbal tea. "This should help you feel a bit better."

"Thanks." Rayne wiped her face with her hands, sniffing.

Anne sipped at her coffee, wondering what Richard had said to Rayne. She also wondered what Rayne was planning to say before Kandi entered the room.

The doorbell rang, and Anne strode out of the dining room to meet Deputy Ruiz. She explained the earlier events, and he and another officer went upstairs. The slamming of a car door outside made Anne think that Carson had arrived, but he'd have to be speeding to get here. She looked out the window.

It was Ivy.

The woman came into the house and was met by the stares of the three women. The song she was singing died on her lips. "What's up with you all? You look like someone just died."

"Where have you been? I needed you!" Rayne rose from her chair.

Taken aback, Ivy replied, "What are you talking

about? You sent me to your apartment because you'd forgotten the earrings you wanted to wear today. I looked everywhere but couldn't find them, so I brought some others."

"I never told you to do that."

"Um, yes, you did. I got a text from you last night telling me to go get them. It was already so late, I stayed at your place until this morning."

"Can anyone vouch for that?" Anne asked.

"The text is on my phone. I can show you that, but why? What's with the third degree?"

"It's Casey."

"Casey? What happened?"

Rayne sprang from her chair. "He tried to kill me, that's all! And she will pay for it. I know they were in it together."

"Whoa. Is this true? Is Casey all right?"

Anne motioned for a shaken-up Ivy to have a seat. "Casey was found unconscious. We don't know what happened. Just in case the officers ask, did anyone see you who can vouch for you?"

Ivy clasped her hands together. "I'm not sure. I guess the people I saw last night and this morning."

Rayne rushed out of the room. "Don't follow me. I want to be alone!" They heard the front door slam behind her.

Ivy's expression verged on the edge of breaking down.

Anne patted her knee. "Don't take Rayne's outburst personally. We don't know yet what happened with Casey. She wasn't doing well when we saw her, though."

"That's horrible," Ivy said. "If only I'd been here. Why does Rayne think it's about her?"

"Casey was wearing her missing dress, and there was a note from Richard. I'm not sure why Rayne didn't drink from the glass this morning."

"Probably because that's when she was out for her jog. She sent me a text that she was going out for a jog this morning to clear her head."

"Can I see your phone?"

"Um, sure." Ivy reached into a pocket of her bag and pulled out her phone. There was a message from Rayne this morning at five that she was going for a jog. She'd be back around seven.

The message before read, Go to my apartment tonight. I forgot my pearl earrings for tomorrow. Will want for photos.

Anne handed the phone back. "That was pretty late when you had to leave."

Ivy smirked. "You don't know Rayne, do you? When she says jump, she wants you to reply, how high? If it wasn't for how well it pays, and because it's for an internship, I wouldn't have taken the job."

"You've been working for her for a while, then?"

Ivy shook her head. "Only a month or so. Rayne said she had this event coming up and needed an extra pair of hands for it to ensure all the details fell into place. After this, I'm on retainer until she no longer needs me, and then I'll be going back to college in the fall."

"Oh, so temporary then?"

"Yes, otherwise, no way I'd keep this job. This event is separate from the internship. But it will help me as she's paying for this herself. "

The door opened and Rayne entered. "I'm sorry for that outburst earlier. I'm so worried about Casey, and now we'll need to call off everything. Ivy, we need to spend some time together. I just need to find my phone."

"You don't have it?"

"No, I must have mislaid it somewhere after this morning. I did that last night, too. Couldn't find it for a while and then there it was. I need one of those tracker thingies on it." She motioned for Ivy to follow, and they left the room.

"Are you thinking what I'm thinking?" Kandi said.

Anne nodded. "Someone else sent that text to Ivy last night. They obviously wanted her out of the way. But who?"

Footsteps on the staircase caused them to look up. Richard stood in the doorway. "Hullo. Hope you don't mind, but I went ahead and stayed in the apartment upstairs last night. Any chance of a cup of coffee?" He scanned their faces. "Am I missing something? I'll pay if I need to for the rental."

"Didn't you hear the ambulance?"

He knit his brows together. "Sorry, what?"

"The sirens? You didn't hear them?"

"No, sorry. I took a sleeping pill and put my

headphones on. I need some white noise to sleep."

Rayne appeared at the door, shrieking, "Murderer!"

After lots of shouting, the quiet after everyone left was substantial. Carson had arrived and quickly worked with Deputy Ruiz to separate the couple, who had started a shouting match with one another. Accusations flew between the pair. Finally, they were advised to separate, with Rayne being asked to go down to the station and give a statement of the events.

Richard went back upstairs as Rayne was escorted out of the cul-de-sac and down to the station, where her statement would be made. Anne faced Kandi—who was barely holding it together, her lip quivering with emotion—and Hope, who hadn't revealed her thoughts. Ivy had gone outside, with her thumbs tapping furiously on her phone.

"Come on, then. Let's go back to the kitchen and think this through." Anne led the way back to the kitchen, which was overflowing with boxes of food and other items. They took their places around the table, and Anne took in a deep breath. "We might as well see what we can salvage food-wise. Kandi, I know you had a lot of things already prepared. What are your thoughts?"

"I could take it over to Family Care Women's Center. I think a lot of it could be eaten today or tomorrow like the cake, bread, and I'm sure they can create casseroles with the chicken and beef. That would count as a donation so could help offset some of the cost."

Hope replied, "Good idea, and it's a great nonprofit, too. We have to face the fact that we probably won't see any more money from the event."

"What about the contract?"

"There's a kill fee—"

"Oh, do we have to use that word?" Kandi replied.

"It still won't cover the cost of all the food, the flowers, and all the items we had to rent to pull this off. Plus, the crews left holes from the various equipment they put in the ground. The grass will need some plugs to fix that."

Hope ran her fingers through her pixie. "This is going to be tough to recover from. Especially if it is reported as food poisoning or something like that. I wouldn't be surprised to have a health inspector show up at any moment and shut us down."

"But we've never had a problem before," Kandi retorted. "I'm very careful."

"I know you are, but this is a big problem." Hope rose from her chair, pacing the room.

Anne knew that she was thinking, so she remained quiet. Would this mean the end of the Brandywine Inn? She was the one who had pushed for the event, and now they'd be going into the red because of her. Tears pricked at her eyes. "I'm sorry. I've really messed things up this time. This is all my fault. I'm just sorry if it reflects badly on either of you. I will take full responsibility, whatever happens."

Hope faced Anne. "While I appreciate you willing to fall on your sword of us, we all agreed to take this on, knowing it was risky. We'll just have to wait to see what happens."

"Okay, so what should we do for now?"

Hope replied, "Well, let's get the food sorted out first. Kandi, keep what we can use in the Inn, and let's get the rest over to the nonprofit. Probably need to call them first. Will you need help with that?"

Kandi grabbed her phone from her pocket. "No, Stewart has a few days free now that he's finished with his last contract. I'll ask if he can come help me."

Anne smiled. "You have him wrapped around your little finger. Of course, he'll help you."

"Great," Hope said. "I'm going to go over the books, see if we can return things earlier. That might help cut costs. I'll see what else we can do to mitigate the damage."

"It sounds like you both have everything in hand here. If it's okay with you, I'm going to re-do one bunch of the flowers and take it up to Casey. I'd like to find out what's happening with her. Did we get the hospital they took her to?"

Kandi answered, "Yes, here you go."

"Okay. Let me get going. I'm not sure they'll let me see her. From what I gathered, it sounded like it was touch and go, so I better call first."

As Kandi called Stewart, Hope left the kitchen,

and Anne called the hospital. She was walking toward the front of the house when she heard the front door open. "Hello?" she called out.

It was Lee Branson. "Hi, sorry to bother you. After everything happened this morning, I think I left a camera lens over at your house."

Lee's countenance was that of despair, and Anne wondered if the incident had impacted him. "Were you, I mean, are you close to Casey?"

His face distorted into pain for a brief second before he composed himself. "Not real close. But she's a good egg. We had lots of fun out on assignments, and she made sure I got good shots. She's always encouraging me to submit my photography for awards. I don't understand this. It makes no sense. There's no way she did anything wrong."

"I agree it seems strange that she worked her shift at the station, then came back here and put on Rayne's dress. What would be the point? And she just took something Rayne believes was meant for her? It's weird."

Anne recalled how Casey had seemed a bit drunk the evening before when they'd spoken. Had she drunk more after she returned?

"Yep. Though she wasn't feeling well last night. She went to the station but once inside, she told them she was ill and would have to skip the news segment," Lee said.

Anne frowned. "She drove to the station, checked in but didn't do the news, and then came back here after that."

In her mind, Anne went over a possible scenario. Maybe Casey had already prepared a drink for Rayne that would cause her to become ill. Then, once she arrived at the station, she realized what she'd done and changed her mind about it, wanting to get back before Rayne took it.

"Lee, what're your thoughts about Richard and Casey?"

He bit his lip for a moment, graying mustache moving with the gesture. He sighed. "It's pretty obvious he and Casey have an attraction. That's why everyone at the station was stunned when Richard started up with Rayne and even more so when they got engaged."

Anne wondered if anyone knew about Rayne's pregnancy but didn't say anything as Lee continued, "I'm so worried about Casey. I hope she pulls through this."

"Me too. But she's got youth and health on her side. I'm going to go up there and visit if you think they'll allow me."

"She's unconscious still, but I think it would be okay if you came with me. After I see if the lens is here, we can drive together."

"I better take my car, so you don't have to come back here. But thanks for the offer." Anne led the way back to her house, and she noticed that many cars were gone, including Richard's. He must have decided to head out.

Lee went up to the top apartment, then came down toting a duffle bag. "Geez, not just the lens but the whole bag. This morning's events really rattled me."

"Am I right that you took a video of them taking Casey away?"

He nodded. "Once a cameraman, always a cameraman. You see any news and it's a habit to record it. I wouldn't be surprised if it's not on the six o'clock and ten o'clock news tonight."

Anne's brow furrowed. Surely not.

He rubbed his hand against his cheek, then used his fingers to pat down his mustache. "Sympathy. People will keep checking in to find out what's going on. Talk online and elsewhere will increase. It's a ratings coup."

"It's disgusting if that's true," Anne responded. "Oh, sorry."

"No need to apologize. I've been disgusted for a long time."

She wanted to ask why he stayed, but it was never easy to walk away from a career. "Lee, does this mean that more reporters from other channels may be coming?"

He shrugged. "I wouldn't put it past them. They'll want a different angle, but it depends on them."

Oh, no. Anne hadn't thought about that. She'd better warn Kandi and Hope to be wary of any reporters snooping around. That would be one headache too many. She walked Lee outside and waved at him before she noticed Mrs. Cole sitting out on her porch. The two women stared at one another.

Well, she's probably happy that everyone's gone. Even if one guest left the Inn on a stretcher. She wouldn't have done anything to cause this, would she have? Anne swiveled upon hearing a door slam. The priest next door was racing outside. He carried a suitcase and threw it in the backseat before backing out of the driveway, rushing off down the street. She turned back, but Mrs. Cole was already going inside. She didn't have to be psychic to know that she was blaming Anne and the Inn for the new neighbors too.

Chapter Six

There was something about hospitals that made you want to turn and run. Whether it was the clinical look of the place, the smells, or the bit of fear that hospitals instilled, Anne had always been reluctant to visit.

Anne found Casey's room number and made her way to the elevator, carrying a vase of peonies and other flowers. She'd had Hope and Kandi sign a get well card as well. After learning that Casey had been transferred to another floor, she returned to the elevator. As she exited, the next door was closing, and she glimpsed the back of a tall man in black. The doors closed, and Anne walked past them to the reception area.

Seeing the room numbers, she turned right and made her way to an open area with the nurse's desk. A woman in blue scrubs and a black bob came out of a room to her left, closing the door behind her.

"Excuse me, I'm looking—"

The nurse glanced at Anne, her face obstructed by a mask and heavy, black-framed glasses. She turned away and moved toward another hallway.

"Geez. You don't need to be rude just because you're in a hurry," Anne said aloud to herself.

She made her way over to the nurse's station, where another woman sat typing on a computer. "Excuse me, I'm looking for Casey Judson's room."

The nurse typed in the name. "Oh, yes. She was recently moved up here. She's in Room 402." She pointed to the room that the other nurse had just vacated.

"Thank you."

Anne made her way to the room, knocking before entering. Casey's face remained pale, and she was hooked up to machines and an IV drip. Anne set the flowers down on a table across from the bed. After sitting by the bed for a bit and checking messages on her phone, she left the room and went back to the nurse's station.

"Has anyone else been to see her? I thought some of her colleagues from the new station would be here. I'd like to speak to them if they're around. Maybe in the cafeteria or—"

"No. She's been unconscious since she was brought in, and so we've had some calls, but no one's visited. Oh, except her priest."

"Priest? Are you sure?"

The woman made a face. "Yes. He just left before you arrived."

"Oh, thanks." Anne flew over to the window but saw no one outside. Was it the priest from across the street? No. What would he be doing in Denver? But he had been speaking to Rayne. Maybe he'd found out and decided to come and visit Casey. She punched in the elevator buttons and made her way down to the lobby. She looked in the cafeteria but didn't recognize anyone. Whoever it was, they were either in another room or had left. Seeing a piece of pie calling her name, she grabbed it, along with a latte. Maybe she'd spot someone she knew from the station while she waited. Satisfied from her snack break, Anne figured she might as well head home to beat the traffic. Anne dug in her purse to grab her phone but realized she'd left it on the window ledge in Casey's room.

Anne waited for the next elevator before tapping in the floor number. After exiting the elevator, she walked toward Casey's room when a nurse stopped her. "I'm sorry, you can't go in there."

"I left my phone when I was visiting Casey. I'll just be a minute." She made to approach the room when the nurse took her arm. "I'm sorry to tell you this, but Miss Judson passed away."

"What? But I was just in there. I mean, mere minutes ago. Are you sure you have the right person?"

She nodded. The nurse led Anne to a seat in a nearby alcove. "Please wait here, and I'll retrieve your phone for you."

Shocked, Anne stared at her hands. They were trembling, and she stilled them by placing them under her thighs. The nurse returned and handed Anne her phone. "May I call someone for you?"

"No, thank you." The nurse left, and Anne steeled herself to leave. Exiting the seating area, she glanced to the door, now busy with the activity of people entering the room.

Anne made her way down to her car, where she sat behind the steering wheel, staring at nothing.

Then the floodgates opened.

Poor Casey. Anne didn't know her, but her life had been cruelly taken from her. And for what? An error in judgment or something else? Had she been the perpetrator or the intended victim all along? And what about the priest who'd been in her room before Anne arrived? If she could speak to him, maybe he would have some answers.

Anne pulled tissues from her purse and blew her nose. She didn't want to call Kandi or Hope but would tell them in person. That would be better.

Hamburgers sizzled on the griddle. Carson flipped one with a deft hand. Anne finished cutting up the tomatoes and laid them out on a platter with the other accoutrements for the burgers.

"Want your bun toasted?" She picked up some buns from a bag.

"Yep, sounds good," he replied.

After he'd finished the burgers, she said, "Want to take these outside or eat in here?"

"Let's just stay in here. I feel that you have a lot on your mind. Want to talk about it?"

"Yes, but not while we're eating. Let's wait until afterwards. Tell me something good that happened today." She smeared some mustard across the crusty bun.

"I talked with Ruiz today about running for the

sheriff's position. He feels honored I'd put my endorsement behind him."

Anne added lettuce, onion, and pickle to her burger, her mind considering Carson's words. "So, you're serious about retiring, then?"

"Yes, I told you. I've seen too many people who didn't realize their days were numbered. Just the other day, I was called to a scene where a motorcyclist cut in front of a truck. He must have thought he could make it." Carson sighed. "Now his family is without him. It's tragic." Carson took Anne's hand. "I never thought I could find happiness and love again like I have with you. I don't want to waste one minute of this gift."

"You may change your mind once you're around me all the time. Plus, I've gotten so used to being on my own, as have you, that I'm not sure how that would work."

"Look, I've been patient, and I know you want to make sure, but we need to commit to this life. Hope told me she thinks you all need to shut down the Inn. That would free up more time for us. There's also the decision of where we'll live. I know you love this old place, but you can't beat the quiet and the stars out at my place. And I know you like the house since you picked out the interior features and colors. So, what is it?"

"I enjoy doing my gardening and consulting. That will be harder out where you live because of the wildlife."

Carson pulled some potato chips from an open

bag and added them to his plate. He stuck one in his mouth, chewing, while he dusted his hands off. He wiped his mouth. "Not a problem. We can either put in caged, raised beds or a greenhouse."

"But what will you do all day if I'm still working?"

"Well, you won't be working all the time. I'd like to do some traveling, and I've actually got an idea for a book."

Anne's expression revealed her amazement. "A book?"

"Don't look so surprised. You know I love reading. I've had some ideas I've jotted down the last few years. I think I have enough for a series of books."

"Wow." Anne sat back in her chair. "I have to say you have surprised me. What type of books?"

"What else? Crime thrillers." He picked up his hamburger and took a bite.

Anne motioned with her finger. "Mustard."

He licked the edge of his lips and smiled at Anne. "So what do ya think? And don't worry about money. I've made smart investments over the years, along with savings, so we wouldn't be in the poorhouse."

"It's a lot to consider. I wouldn't mind doing some traveling, and it would give me time to work on a book I've considered doing on gardening plans. I promise I'll think about it."

He finished chewing before he spoke again. "I want us to set a date. Soon."

Anne laughed. "I thought we weren't going to get into serious matters while we were eating."

He took her hand. "I am serious, Anne. We love each other. I love you. If you said let's go right now and get married, I'd do it."

"I love you—"

"Here comes the 'but' again. What's the problem?"

"I've been giving thought to housing and lots of other things. Now, with everything going on with the Inn, I have to focus. I cost us a lot of money by taking this risk with this event. My focus has to be there."

Carson's face grew dark. "Anne—"

Luckily, she was saved by the trilling of her phone. It was Rayne. "I have to take this." She stood. "Hi Rayne. I'm so sorry about—" She spied Carson telling her to put it on speaker. She complied.

"I didn't know if you had heard the news about Casey. It's horrible. We're all in shock here, as you can imagine."

"Yes, I went up to the hospital today. I was there..." She didn't complete the sentence.

"It's tragic. To be honest, we weren't that close. It was basically a work friendship."

Anne frowned. Whether or not they'd been close, Rayne's response was pretty callous.

"As you can imagine, upper management considers this a big news story. We want to come by in the next few days with the camera crew and do some shots of the Inn, get a few statements from you and the others who were there—"

Carson shook his head, and Anne replied, "I'm not

73

sure that would be a good idea."

Rayne's melodious voice carried through the speaker. "No worries. We can speak to some neighbors."

That was the last thing Anne wanted. "I'm sure we can figure something out but not sure we can provide any information. Changing subjects, how are you feeling now about what you said the other day?"

"I gather you mean about Richard? It came as a huge shock finding Casey barely breathing and in my wedding dress. I've been wracking my brain about it. I think it was Casey I saw the first day out in the garden. There's been so much going on here at the studio with some silly pranks, but Casey had them happen to her as well. It never dawned on me she may have been doing them herself."

"I still don't see why either of them would do anything at this point."

"What do you mean?"

"Well, because you're already married to Richard."

Rayne shrieked, "Who told you that?"

Anne didn't want to get Ivy in trouble, so she responded, "I can't remember where I heard it."

Rayne groaned. "Yes, it's true. We were married a few months ago. That's why I think Richard and Casey were trying to frighten ...or even kill me. We took out insurance policies right after we were married. Plus, it's no secret around the station that Casey's been eyeing my job from day one. I haven't given notice or stepped down, and polls don't mean anything. You can skew them however you want. At least that's one thing I won't have to worry about now." Rayne caught herself. "Sorry, I know that sounds harsh after everything that's happened, but—well, I guess we'll find out soon enough what they think happened."

Anne looked at her burger, getting colder by the minute, when a thought came to her. "Rayne, I saw a tall man in a dark suit visit Casey just before—"

"I know Richard said he was going up to visit her and see if there was any change."

"Oh, maybe that's who I saw. For some reason, I thought it was the priest from across the street." There was silence on the line. "Rayne, are you there?"

"Um, yes. I'm not sure who you're referring to, so I can't help you."

"It was the man you spoke with the night of the reception dinner."

Rayne laughed. "Oh, yes, him. Sorry, I didn't catch his name. I can't remember what he was doing there. Something about a blessing or something...you know how it is, things are so confused right now."

"Sure. Well, if there's not anything else—"

"Oh, one last thing. I've heard you're a bit of an amateur sleuth yourself."

Anne spied Carson give her a knowing look of 'don't get involved.' "Not really. Just figured some things out. That's all."

"I'd like to sit down with you for an interview about your gardening and all of that. Maybe we could set up something next week."

"Okay, that sounds fine."

"All right then. We can work out the details tomorrow." The line went dead.

Carson pointed a finger at Anne. "Don't even think about it."

"What? It's just an interview." But inside, Anne was already thinking there was one person she really needed to talk to, and he lived across the street. What had the priest been saying to Rayne that evening, and why had he come over to their party? Was it Richard or the priest she'd seen leaving Casey's room shortly before her death?

Chapter Seven

Birds chirping outside her window woke Anne. By the time Carson had left in the evening, a somber mood had settled over them. Neither was willing to go any further with the earlier conversation, but it hung heavy between them. Anne also didn't bring up the events at the Inn as that would tie in with so many other conversations. So, they'd rocked on the glider on the front porch until Carson had kissed her good night and left.

Mouser pounced up on the bed, meowing. Anne picked him up and looked in his eyes. "What would you do in my situation, Mouser? It's not like I can just flip a coin or something. Plus, you're used to this house. Would you want to go live somewhere else?"

He meowed, but it was more of a 'put me down, woman' sound. "Fine. You're no help." She set him down, and he kneaded the bedspread before curling up in a ball next to her. It felt funny not to have to get up and get busy with the day's events. The Inn was effectively closed for the next few days at least, and they had grayed out the reservation calendar for the time being. Anne dreaded having to talk with Hope and Kandi about everything that needed to be discussed, especially how much they were in the hole now.

She sighed and turned to face Mouser, running

her hands along his black fur. His purring grew louder. "At least you're not upset with me."

Her phone beeped. She reached back to the nightstand and opened the drawer. It was Kandi: Hey off with Stewart today. Heading to Estes for a bit of a break. Chat later. Love ya. She'd finished it with a line of hearts and emojis.

Well, that was good to hear. Kandi had been spending all her time at the Inn preparing for the event, and Anne knew Stewart must be feeling like Carson about being ignored. She knew Kandi was realizing how much Stewart loved her, and Anne was sure they'd end up together. Like Anne, Kandi had gone through some healing herself when it came to relationships.

Why couldn't anything be easy? Anne dropped the phone back into the charging tray and closed the drawer.

Well, with Kandi off, that meant that she wouldn't be there for the news interviews. That would be one blessing in all of this. Hope had retreated back to her place, and so Anne would face any issues that arrived today. But first, a good cup of java was in order. Yawning and stretching, she took her time getting ready before padding downstairs to put on the coffee pot. After the steaming hot brew was ready, she took her cup and made her way outside to the front porch.

Across the road, Mr. Cole was outside working trimming his hedges, and he responded with a wave when he saw her.

Well, at least he didn't hold any animosity toward her. Maybe she could get him to speak to his wife. As if on cue, Mrs. Cole came through the door. Anne waved at the woman, who returned it half-heartedly.

Maybe they could work things out after all. She sipped at her coffee, turning over her next steps in her mind. Best to be ready with some prepared answers in case the news crew showed up early. Yet it was difficult, if not impossible, to prepare for unknown questions. She'd have to keep things general and see if that would work. For now, she had to present them as having no fault in any of what occurred.

By the time the news van pulled up, Anne felt a bit better about answering questions concerning the Inn and its past. Rayne had driven her own car, and they began with shots of the Inn and the back yard. Because Rayne was, in essence, part of the story itself, she never appeared on camera, voicing questions from the side that would be edited out. Her co-host would appear to ask some questions on camera, with Anne's responses shown. She was glad Lee was the cameraman as she felt at ease with him being there.

Rayne asked some basic questions about how long the Inn had been running, and Anne replied with great form, including many of the recommendations they'd received from guests from all over the country. When Rayne finally touched on the incident with Casey, Anne stuck to what she'd rehearsed. It appeared to be a tragic accident, but it was in the hands of capable law enforcement now. As Rayne continued to push harder,

Anne realized the woman was trying to provoke her into getting angry or saying something she'd regret. But Anne refused to be goaded into making a mistake and stayed on course. When Rayne finally said she thought they'd gotten enough footage, Anne took in a deep breath of relief.

As Rayne strode away, taking a phone call, Lee said, "Good on you. Most people break down. I think she met her match with you."

"I felt on trial for a bit, but I guess she wanted something a little more newsworthy. I have to say, she doesn't seem broken up about Casey or Richard."

He lowered his camera to his side. "You've got good perception. She and Casey, if anything, were frenemies. They made nice for the cameras, but I don't think either of them could stand each other. Of course, Casey gunning for Rayne's prime spot didn't help."

Anne faced away in case Rayne could see what she said. "Then doesn't it seem weird that she had Casey as her maid of honor?"

"No. More publicity for them. 'BFFs for the cameras'." He made air quotes with his fingers. "And of course, Rayne knew that Casey and Richard had dated a few times. Still not sure who ended that."

Anne asked, "What about Richard? I mean, if Rayne honestly believes he was trying to kill her, shouldn't she be more upset? I know I would be."

"Rayne is all about the ratings. You can believe she'll use the footage and the photos of the event to her benefit to make everyone feel sorry for her. I guess

Richard will hire lawyers, and there'll be a nice, big settlement of some sort, along with an NDA."

"But what about the baby?"

Lee's brow furrowed. "What baby?"

Anne looked over to where Rayne was still speaking into her phone, wildly gesturing with her free right hand. Somebody on the other end of that call was getting an earful.

"Rayne's pregnant."

Lee burst out laughing. "I don't think so. That woman doesn't have a maternal bone in her body. She wouldn't allow the 'indignity' of losing her figure or the effect on her career. No. I don't know who told you that, but it's simply not true."

"Maybe she's changed. Or she, you know, had to get married."

Lee shook his head. "This isn't the last century. Things have changed now. No, I'll never believe she's pregnant or that it was the reason Richard married her."

"Why would Ivy say that, then?"

"Who knows? She's just a kid—an overworked one for sure, working for Rayne. But with everything that's happened, she's been let go. So, she's back to enjoying a college break before the next semester."

As Rayne ended her call, Lee took up his camera and started filming her. As soon as she noticed his lens focused on her, her very demeanor and posture changed. She made it over to them and put out her hand to shake Anne's.

"Ugh, I had a spot all planned out, and now we're going to have to think about replacing it with something else. Hey, I have an idea. Why don't you do a gardening spot for our viewers? I think they'd love hearing about your stuff, and we'd promote your books. What do you say? It could be a bit of a test run. If we get helpful feedback, we could do one to two spots every month."

Anne's eyes lit up. "Well, I, um, that sounds fun. But I'd need to think about it."

"Well, don't wait too long. We'll need to fill that spot soon, and chances like this don't come along very often."

"I will. Thank you for thinking of me."

"Sure. Lee, I'm heading back. If you need anything else, you can text me."

She sashayed off to her vehicle without a goodbye.

"Well, that's exciting." Anne smiled at Lee, who had a worried look on his face.

"Be careful."

"What do you mean?"

"I don't know. Just a gut feeling, I guess." He strode back to the van, leaving Anne with more questions.

Anne had climbed the steps to the front porch when the door swung open, and the biker appeared.

"Oh, hey," he said. "Sorry, I was just on my way

out. Can I help you?"

"Yes, I was looking for the priest. Is he in?"

"Priest? Oh, you mean Dean."

Anne nodded. "Yes, Dean. Is he home?"

The biker shrugged. "Not sure. He's at the theater most evenings for rehearsals and sleeps in most days. But I haven't seen him around lately."

"Oh, well, I—"

"Wait, are you with the recent production? I couldn't believe he got such a sweet gig for that amount of money. Oh, man, I wonder if he already left."

It was hard to keep up with the young man's train of thought. "Left?"

"Yep, to Mexico. Some gig down there after this one."

Anne thought fast. Obviously, he didn't realize he was speaking to a neighbor. She replied, "That boy. No call his mother before he left—"

"Oh, you're his mom?" He held out his hand for her to shake.

She accepted his hand while thinking *it doesn't count as a lie if I didn't say it, right*? Her conscience elbowed her, but she ignored it. She needed to get into his apartment. "I guess I'll have to wait until he gets back then." She let out a long sigh.

"Oh, do you need something? The doors inside aren't locked, or if they are, there are spare keys on a hook in the kitchen. Listen, I gotta run so I can get my ride in before getting ready for work." He pulled his bike out the door, leaving it open. "Bye!"

Anne starred after him as he rode off toward the trailhead. "Geez, I could have been an axe murderer. Kids these days." She laughed at her remark about someone who was most likely in his twenties.

Now she had to decide. Should she shut the door or go on and search Dean's room? Carson's face and his admonition of 'don't do it' came to mind, but she convinced herself this could be the clue they needed to figure out what really happened to Casey. She stepped inside and listened. She could hear some music coming from a closed door to her left. She peeked in and saw another roommate playing a game on the big screen in the corner. His back was to her, and she closed the door with a quiet touch. Taking the stairs, she realized she wouldn't have any idea which room was Dean's. She knocked on the first one. When there was no answer, she opened the door to a bed strewn with clothing as a wave of eau de male sweat hit her.

"Ugh." She put up a hand to cover her nose and mouth. A shelf held trophies and ribbons with medallions. This must be the biker's room. She closed the door and went over to the door adjacent to his.

She knocked again. When there wasn't an answer, she cracked open the door. This room contained a loft bed with a desk underneath it. College books and papers littered the floor and chairs. This was most likely the person downstairs, as some game stickers adorned a laptop backpack slung over the edge of the bed's railing.

"Hopefully, third time's the charm." She made her way across the hall to another closed door. After knocking, she peeked inside and, seeing Dean's name on a wall plaque, entered the space, shutting the door behind her. Unlike his roommates, Dean's space was clean and organized. Also, thankfully, not reeking of male lack of hygiene. Riffling through the desk drawers, she came across pay stubs from the local coffee shop, playbills from the theatre in town, and a listing of upcoming productions. Some were circled in red pen. Anne looked at the list. Auditions for a local commercial, upcoming events requiring extras, and some personal ads. She scanned them quickly, then gasped as one stood out.

Play a priest. Must have a costume. Great pay for easy work. Opportunity for bonus.

Had he been playing a priest for Rayne and Richard's 'wedding' performance? It made sense, as they were already married, so they didn't need a real pastor or priest to officiate the ceremony. But for him to live across the street—that was some coincidence.

Anne set the paper down and took a photo of the ad with her phone. She replaced it and looked around the room. Maybe that was why the room was so tidy. Maybe Dean had only moved in for a short duration. She crossed over to the closet. Empty.

She couldn't imagine him taking all his clothing with him on his trip. There was definitely something going on here, but did it have anything to do with the incident at the Inn? Plus, had he been at the hospital or was it Richard she'd seen that day?

Just as she decided to leave, she got down on her knees to look under the bed.

Eureka. It was the priest's collar. She pulled a tissue from her purse before taking the collar, wrapping it up, and placing it inside her bag. What she would do with it she did not know, but she could always return it later.

Taking one more glance around the room, she backed out, closing the door behind her when a hand clamped down on her shoulder.

Chapter Eight

Anne screamed, throwing his hand off her shoulder with a violent twist. The young man, shocked at her scream, lurched backward, falling through the door to his room. A bowl he held with soup splattered over him, along with the wall and Anne.

"What's the matter with you, lady?" he cried.

Anne bent down. "Oh, I'm so sorry. I ...you scared me."

He sat, pushing what was left of his ramen off his shirt. "I scared you? You're not the one covered in soup. Man, I was really looking forward to that, too."

Anne held out her hand, "I'm sorry. I didn't—well, are you okay?"

"Yeah. Like, next time, say something first." He wiped his hands on his damp shirt. "What were you doing in Dean's room?"

Anne thought fast. "I'm his mother."

His face scrunched in thought. "I thought his mom lived in Philly."

"Came for a visit but found out he's not here." She shrugged.

He stared at her. "He's in Mexico."

"Yes, silly me. I thought I'd surprise him."

That must have made sense as the young man nodded. "Oh, okay." He reached for his phone. "I can call him."

"No!" Anne laid her hand on his. "It would only make him feel bad that he's not here. Plus, then he wouldn't be surprised next time."

He cocked his head. "Hey, you look kinda familiar. Do I know you from somewhere?"

"Family genes. Dean looks a lot like his mother."

"Ah, okay, that's probably it."

"Listen, I have to run, but how about I order you some takeout since I ruined your lunch? It's the least I can do."

His eyes lit up, and after he'd ordered everything but the kitchen sink from a local restaurant, Anne bid him goodbye. As she made her way downstairs, he stood at the top.

"Oh, one last thing. I thought Dean had moved to another place, closer to Denver, to be near the theaters."

He shrugged. "Don't know about that, but he only rented his room for a month. We have a new roommate next month."

"Oh, so this is short-term rentals?"

"Nah. Dean was upset he had to rent for a full month—that was the least amount of time—but then he said he was getting the money back from what sounded like a really nice acting gig. Then he got that bonus."

"The trip to Mexico?"

"Yep, lucky dog. All-inclusive resort for two weeks. I need to find something like that."

"Well, thanks again."

"Hal."

"Hal?"

He laughed. "That's my name. Hal."

"Oh, gotcha. Again, let's keep this between us. I want to surprise Dean."

"Will do." He retreated from the landing without saying another word.

"And goodbye to you too." Anne skipped down the front porch steps and looked back from the street to ensure Hal wasn't watching. The last thing she needed was for him to see her go back across the street and put two and two together.

As she made sure the coast was clear, her gaze caught the curtains falling back in the upstairs window of the Coles' house. Had one of the Coles been watching her? She sprinted across the street before anyone else saw her. Going around the back to her house, her phone pinged with a text.

It was Rayne: Want to chat about interview. Also, opportunity for your weekly spot on the show.

Anne texted back: Sounds good. Let me know when you'd like to chat.

When no return reply came, she tucked the phone away and made her way up to her back steps. Inside, she sat down and thought about what she should do with the collar she'd found. It didn't mean anything besides that he was paid to act like a priest. Other than Rayne speaking to him, she had no proof that he'd even worked for her at all.

She drummed her fingers on the table, thinking.

Mouser came through the door and, with great ease of movement, landed lightly on the table where he began licking his paw. "Mouser, what do you think I should do with this information?"

He kept licking his paw.

"A lot of good you are. I need some help here." That was it. She needed to have a talk with Hope and Kandi. They always had good ideas.

She texted them about coming over later for dinner. Kandi noted that she and Stewart had planned for dinner there, but she could come afterward. Another text arrived. Hope noted that she had to do some restocking and would just grab something before coming over as well.

Anne texted: Okay. See you then.

She put down her phone. What should she do in the meantime? A timeline would be good to have on hand while they all talked about the events. She could do it on paper, but better to use the whiteboard in the office. She picked up her things and made her way across to the Inn. It seemed so weird for it to be closed up without people coming and going. She unlocked the back door and let herself in.

Before starting on the timeline, she went over to the coffeemaker and made herself a hazelnut latte. After she'd added the milk foam to the top, she sprinkled a dusting of cinnamon. She hoped it wouldn't cause problems sleeping tonight. After she'd cleaned the machine's frother, she went back into the office. She'd taken a sip of the hot, sweet brew when she remembered about the ducks. She opened the door to spy the ducklings cuddled up together, napping. Her presence made them open their eyes, and their beaks flapped with cute quacking noises.

"I see Kandi has you trained to know who gives the treats." She pulled some treats out of a bag sitting near the sink and put them down in the tub. Some of the ducklings were growing fairly quickly, and she wondered how long before Kandi would need to move them into their permanent quarters. She refilled their water container before going back into the office.

Where should I start? She wrote TIMELINE in caps at the top and drew a line under it. Then, realizing they'd want to see where people were during the timeline, she erased it and moved it over to the left side of the whiteboard.

Using a black erasable marker, Anne wrote:

Day 1 (Pre-event) TV crew and others arrive for set-up.

Day 2 (Reception Dinner evening)

·Rayne arrives with Richard.

·Photographers take pictures of them arriving

·Cameramen on scene (Lee and others)

·Casey arrives

·Ivy on scene telling everyone about the night's events (Side note: Rayne not with group)

·Rayne comes running in, says she saw someone wearing her wedding dress, dead.

·Hope and I look around. Nothing. Find a snippet of lace.

·Wedding dress (one of many!) missing from her dressing room. Not found after search.

Day 2 (Reception Dinner)

·Rayne and Richard meet guests as they arrive (side note: where was Ivy during that time?)

·Priest speaks to Rayne behind bushes (side note: was it Dean or someone else?)

·Dinner (Kandi to confirm nothing could have been tampered with as to cause food poisoning)

·Casey excuses herself to go to sleep. (side note: drunk?)

·Everyone leaves

·Richard stays in the attic apartment, per Rayne's request (side note: was it because she was afraid?)

·Richard goes upstairs, takes sleeping pills, and puts on headphones. Goes to sleep (side note: how many pills were in bottle and how many the next morning? Did Rayne take any pills? Need to ask her.)

·Rayne goes to bed (unsure of what happened after that point)

·Casey says she needs to catch a few winks because she has to leave early for the morning show (unknown if she went to sleep or not)

·Ivy leaves to drive back to Denver to get Rayne's jewelry. Says she stayed in Denver.

·Kasey leaves in the morning to drive into Denver for show (side note: car was back when I woke up.)

Day 3 (morning after the dinner)

·Rayne has been throwing up. Ivy with her (side note: if Ivy did stay in Denver, when did she get back?)

·Find Casey in Rayne's wedding dress, barely alive.

·Call EMTs.

·Rayne comes downstairs. Says it was an attack on her life.

·Deputy Ruiz arrives. They go upstairs.

·Richard comes downstairs. Says he spent the night there.

·Casey taken to hospital.

·Richard (or priest?) visits Casey (side note: find out when Dean left for Mexico)

·Casey dies.

Anne stood back and looked over the timeline. She thought she'd captured all the facts. Now to see if Hope or Kandi remembered anything she'd forgotten. Her phone rang. It was Carson.

"Hey you. What are you up to?"

His warm voice came through the speakers. "Unboxing the lighting. Stewart's going to help me hang some of these things and put on the plug covers, etc. It'll save me waiting on the electrician and help Stewart with a little money for his troubles."

"If Kandi would marry that love-sick man, he'd never have to worry about money again." Anne chuckled.

"Yeah, too bad you don't have someone leaving you millions of dollars. I'd be a happy man." Carson referred to the large inheritance that would soon be Kandi's.

"Well, I'm way over the age she needed to be to

collect the money, plus I know for a fact money doesn't mean that much to you."

"You got me there. I like it, but I don't want to sell my soul to get it."

"Hmm, I wonder if Richard would, though."

"I thought his family had an estate in England or something or other."

Anne responded, "Maybe he's one of those house and land rich but money-poor people."

"Could be a possibility, I guess."

"So, what's going on with the case?"

"N.D.!"

She waffled between being angered by his pet name for her and touched. "I'm only asking a question."

"Obviously, Miss Judson's death is suspicious. But that's all I can say now. Ruiz is taking the lead, so I'm out of the loop on it unless he needs my input."

Anne huffed. "Well, that's no help!"

He laughed. "No help to who—you?"

"Let's talk about something else."

"Yes, lets. How about something good?"

"Rayne wants to talk to me about a weekly spot on the news. Kind of like a lifestyle feature."

Instead of the expected congratulations, she was met with stony silence.

"Hello? Carson, you there?"

His voice was lowered. "Yes, I'm here."

"What do you think? I'm pretty excited. This could be a fantastic opportunity for me. Imagine what kind of impact it could have on my future."

"Your future? What about our future?"

"I, um—"

Vitriol flew through the phone such as she'd never heard from him. "I see how it is. Everything's fine as long as things go on the same as they are now. Until we discuss 'our' future, I don't think there's anything we have to say to each other."

"What are you saying?"

"I'm saying..."

"What?" Anne clutched the phone tighter.

"Maybe a break is a good thing right now. Give you some time to decide what you want for your future. I gotta go."

Anne stared at the phone. He hadn't said I love you or given her a chance to respond. A wave of emotion overtook her as she slipped into the office chair, laid her head on the desk, and wept.

Chapter Nine

Since she had some time before she met with Kandi and Hope, Anne went home and drew a hot bath. She added lavender to the water, and as she lowered herself into the tub, she prayed that the heat would bring healing to her broken heart. Tears trickled down her face as she thought over her last conversation with Carson.

She had grown so used to everything being about herself that she'd neglected thinking of them, or as he'd noted, the focus was on her versus them , her versus their future. Had she ruined one of the best things in her life? She laid her head back against the porcelain tub edge, willing herself to relax. Taking deep breaths, she allowed her mind to wander. Finally, as the water cooled, she pulled herself from the tub, wrapping herself in a large terrycloth towel.

Her phone beeped, signaling that she'd exited the tub just before the timer went off. She'd texted Hope and Kandi about meeting at the Inn to discuss recent events.

After dressing in a pair of comfy leggings and an over-sized T-shirt, she shucked into some sneakers before grabbing Mouser, who was trying his escape act through the back door. "I've told you repeatedly, there are much bigger cats out there that would eat you for a snack. Stay inside, or you'll be dinner for some creature out there, mister."

Living in the Colorado mountains, it wasn't unusual for mountain lions, black bears, elk, even an occasional moose to be seen at the edge of her yard. Since the wildlife lived there long before Carolan Springs was developed, she respected them, and thankfully, they kept their distance as well.

Mouser meowed his affront at her stopping him from leaving but was assuaged when she tipped a few treats into his bowl. As he munched on the treats, she closed the door behind her. Already, she could see a light on in the Inn's office. She walked over and found Kandi constructing a plate of nachos. She pulled a tray of some lemon cookies from the oven.

"I thought you went out to eat?"

"Stewart said Carson needed some more help with the lights and asked for a raincheck on dinner for tonight. We already spent the day together, so I'm fine with that. I figured you hadn't eaten either. So, easy peasy, nachos."

"Did he say anything else to you?"

Kandi cocked her head in an oh-so-familiar motion, causing tears to prick at Anne's eyes.

"What's going on? Has something happened?"

The door opened, and Hope appeared. She scanned their faces. "Did I interrupt something?"

"Anne's upset. Come on, Mom, tell us what's up."

Anne sniffed, touched by Kandi's use of the word mom. It felt like a warm hug to her. She steeled herself. "It's nothing. I—"

Hope replied, "We know you too well. Spit it out."

"I really don't want to talk about it right now. I appreciate you two caring about me, but it's something I need to work through on my own. Plus, I don't want to get sidetracked on why we're here. Okay?"

"Fine, but you better tell us later." Kandi sprinkled cilantro over the nachos. "These are ready. Oh, and here's another tray sans cilantro for you, Hope."

"Thanks. I can't stand that soapy taste. Plus, I'm starving. I had a protein bar, but that's not going to hold me for long." Hope grabbed a chip, the cheese stretching away from the others.

"Yes, thanks Kandi. You always take such good care of us. By the way, how much longer are you keeping the ducks in the bathtub? I think they're getting their feathers, and at the rate they're growing, I can't see them being able to stay in there too much longer."

"I decided not to keep them. After learning how messy they are with the water, and having to refill the tub all the time, I don't think ducks are for me. I can still use the eggs from my chickens, and if I want to get some duck eggs, I can buy them."

"I know you have your hands full with all the cooking for the Inn and everything else."

Kandi's earrings swayed as she nodded in agreement. "You know, sometimes what you think is going to work isn't reality at all."

Anne said, "What did you say?"

Kandi repeated herself. "Did I say something wrong?"

"No, no. I don't know why that's resonating with me. It just is. Maybe it will come to me later."

Hope laughed. "Hopefully, not at two in the morning!"

"Agreed. I hate when that happens, and it takes me a while to convince my brain to go back to sleep. I don't remember it doing that when I was younger."

Hope wiped her hands on a napkin. "Let's go look at what you've got on the whiteboard and see if it makes sense to us. What is it again?"

"Basically, the timeline. So, just the facts. I didn't put actual times, but we can add that if you think we need to do it. I jotted down some notes if something came to me as I was writing."

"Okay, let's go take a look-see."

The trio went into the office, where Anne stood back as Kandi and Hope read her notes on the board.

Kandi said, "Seems like something's missing."

"What is it?" Anne replied.

Kandi bounced with excitement. "Oh, I know. Ivy going back to Denver to get Rayne's jewelry."

"Good catch." Anne added it to the board along with 'Stayed overnight at Rayne's in Denver.'

"Do we know if she stayed overnight, or is that only what she said?" Hope asked.

Anne thought for a moment. "You're right. She could have come back here without any of us knowing it."

Hope sat down at the desk and moved papers out of the way. "Okay, so that leaves the following people in the house when the incident occurred. First, there's Rayne, then Casey, who left but returned later, Richard, who says he took sleeping pills and didn't hear anything, and Ivy, possibly, who left but could have returned to the Inn."

"Got it." Hope took out a piece of paper and drew four lines. At the top, she listed all four names. "We need to look at each of them for means, motive, and opportunity."

Anne nodded. "Agreed. Who should we start with?"

"Let's start with Ivy. She certainly had the means. She was all over the place, and I doubt anyone paid attention to her."

"That establishes some of the means, but what about the pills? Did Rayne have pills, or was it even pills in the glass? Could it have been something else?"

"I hate not knowing what the actual cause of death was. Was it because of something that occurred here or unrelated? We need to find that out." Anne made a note on another slip of paper.

Kandi said, "Okay, so let's say she had the means. What would be, like, her motive? I talked to her, and this job was only for a short time. She needed the recommendation that Rayne could give her."

"Maybe Rayne told her she wasn't giving her a good reference or even that she was going to report it to her school. This could have been part of an internship."

Anne said, "I never thought of that. That actually has some merit to it. Let's see—she gets mad at Rayne making her drive all the way back to Denver for the jewelry. On the way back, she gets angrier. Then she decides to make Rayne pay by giving her something in her drink. Maybe just to make her sick or sleepy. Then she says she arrived that morning. We were all so busy, I doubt any of us knew who was coming or going."

"I know someone who could, like, probably tell us." Kandi motioned with her head toward the cul-de-sac.

At first, it made no sense. Then it dawned on Anne who Kandi had been referring to with her motion.

"Oh, no. We'll have to pick straws to see who talks to Mrs. Cole about it. But let's think about that later," Anne replied.

Hope put a checkmark next to Ivy's name. "Okay, she had means, motive, and opportunity. Who next?"

"Casey, I think. If she still loved Richard, there are two possible explanations of what happened."

"You don't think—"

"I'm not thinking anything. I'm simply asking the questions. We don't know about the means, but we can discuss the motive. We have two scenarios. She meant to kill Rayne, or she meant to take the pills herself."

"I don't see it. Why would she do that?"

"She'd been to the studio. Being wound up and after driving here, she knew she only had a short window to get some sleep. Let's say that she took a couple of sleeping pills. Then maybe she forgot and took some more or had a drink, which is a big no-no with medication. She had definitely been drinking enough for me to notice it the night of the incident. Let's make another timeline separate from her." Anne rose and drew another timeline next to the first one.

Day of Reception Dinner

·*Casey arrives. Goes up to change.*
·*Rayne says there's a dead body wearing her dress. We go out to look and no one's there.*
·*Wedding dress missing.*
·*Dinner guests start arriving.*
·*Casey's at dinner with the others. Appears fine.*
·*Says she's going to bed because she has an early morning.*
·*Goes upstairs.*
·*Unknown what occurs during this time.*
·*Leaves to head to studio. Clocks in but says she's ill.*
·*Returns (time unknown).*
·*Rayne ill. Ivy with her?*
·*Discover Casey unconscious in the dressing room instead of her own room.*

"Does this look correct?" Anne faced Kandi and Hope, who nodded to the affirmative.

Kandi said, "I think so. This timeline leaves us

with, like, a lot of unanswered questions. First, could the person wearing Rayne's dress have been Casey? Maybe she wanted to, like, prank Rayne since she knew Rayne was already on edge about the deaths that had happened here. She could have lain on the grass, then once Rayne saw her, booked it to over to my house. She knew no one was over there as we'd already talked earlier about me living next door. She could have taken off the dress, hidden it, or put it in a suitcase, and, like, no one would be the wiser."

Anne replied, "Possibly. But she had no way of knowing Rayne would run away or that she'd be alone. Sounds like a big gamble to me. And I didn't see any daggers from her eyes at Rayne—or Richard, for that matter. She was more matter-of-fact about the whole thing. I don't think she was that upset about their wedding, to be honest."

Hope went over to the whiteboard. "I think it would be good if we go through each of these bullet points you've done."

"Okay, I'll take notes." Anne went over behind the desk and sat in the office chair, pulling a yellow legal pad toward her and clicking a pen. "Fire when ready."

"I don't think there's any dispute on the first one. We agree on everyone arriving and being shown upstairs."

Kandi nodded. "I took Casey up to her room, so I can vouch for that. She asked where Rayne's room was, though, now that I think about it."

"Great. I'll make a note about it. Sometimes it's a

minor detail that turns into something major later." Anne marked Kandi's note down on the paper.

"Okay, this one may take more time. As far as I recall, the crew gathered downstairs, and Ivy gave some instructions. Most likely on behalf of Rayne."

"Yes, so that means Ivy was inside with everyone when Rayne said there was a body in her dress outside."

Anne tapped the pen on the desk. "Do you remember if Casey was there?"

"I don't remember as I was going back and forth to the kitchen. Though I thought I saw her there, or maybe it was when she was upstairs."

Hope responded, "Yes, I think so too, but I can't recall either. There was so much going on everywhere. I could have seen her before that and just assumed she was there when Ivy was talking."

"Okay, so question mark for where Casey was during that time." Anne wrote on the pad. "We know Rayne went outside by herself to look and see if everything was ready to go."

Kandi hopped up and walked around. "That means she was the only one to, like, see the dead body. We need to QTP."

"QTP?"

Kandi nodded. "Question the premise." She held up her index finger, counting off. "One, what did she see? Two, who did she see? And three, why was she the only one to see it?"

"Ah, good points." Hope erased part of the

whiteboard and wrote QTP at the top. "Let's start with your first question. She said she saw a body that looked like her in her wedding dress. When we got there, there was no sign of a body."

"Wait, we have to stick to the first question. Rayne saw a dead body, she thought she saw a dead body, or..."

"She's lying," Kandi finished Anne's sentence.

"Good points. Let's take them one by one. She saw a dead body. Someone ...and let's say for now it was Casey as she looks the most like Rayne and we're not sure of her whereabouts...was the body. Was it to frighten Rayne, as a prank, or what else could it be?"

"Rayne is all about publicity. Maybe she had someone help her pull off a stunt she could use for more ratings."

"Do you think she'd really do something like that? I don't know. I'm not convinced. When she came in, she practically fainted in Richard's arms."

"Okay, we can rule out number two because there was a scrap of lace from her dress that went missing."

"True, but when the dress was found on Casey, it didn't show any signs of being on the grass. There would have been dirty spots if nothing else."

"Good point. So could it have been a different dress that looked like her wedding gown?"

"Possibly."

"Okay, I'll make a question on that." Anne wrote 'different dress?'

"So, to our last idea, she could have been lying and

put the lace on the branch herself."

The other two nodded.

"What would be, like, the purpose?" Kandi asked.

"Good question. You know, There were other photographers around then. Maybe she wanted to start some kind of rumor."

"Like?"

Kandi used a hand to swipe the air above her. "How about 'Ghostly bride signals tragedy'?"

"Definitely something for the tabloids. But I'm not convinced."

"Okay, so anything else on that question?" Hope asked.

"Nope," Anne and Kandi chimed.

"Okay, so the next question is 'who' did she see? She said she saw a dead body. She didn't say if it was male or female, but we'll assume for the sake of this exercise it was a woman who resembled her."

"That would definitely be Casey. Um, let me think." Kandi snapped her fingers. "You know, Ivy could have put on a wig and played the part."

"But Ivy was inside talking to the crew."

"Oh, yeah. Bummer."

"That makes me think of something, though."

Hope faced Anne. "What?"

Anne shared about Dean, the priest, and his acting. "What if Rayne got someone to act out the part?"

"What about, like, a mannequin?"

Anne chuckled at Kandi. "Remember that old

movie with the mannequin that came to life?"

Kandi's face let Anne know she had no clue to what movie she was referring.

"Before your time. But anyway, as much as I'd say that's ridiculous, we can't rule anything out, so I'll add it to our list."

"Anyone or anything else on the 'who' question?"

"I think we're good. It was Casey, someone unknown, a mannequin supplied by someone hiding who whisked it away after Rayne screamed and ran back inside, or Rayne imagined it."

"Or it could have been something else."

"Such as?"

Kandi shivered. "It was really a ghost."

Anne sighed. "Oh, bother."

"You said we can't, like, rule anything out."

"Okay, fine. I'm writing it down but only under duress."

"No, it's not about the dress."

"Duress, not dress."

"Well, why didn't you say so, then?"

Anne's mouth gaped before she closed it, trying to hide her chuckling. "Let's move on. Why was she the only one to see it? I think we've somewhat answered it, but what else can we consider?"

Hope asked, "What if Richard got Casey to do it? Maybe they wanted to set it up so that Rayne looked like a kook saying she saw something and then we all go out there and nothing's there."

"Hmm, that is an idea. According to Rayne, he

took out a big life insurance policy on her. Richard's face every time he saw Casey had love written all over it. He probably didn't even realize it was so evident," Anne said.

"Love triangles never go well. Especially when people also work together, and one is vying for the other's job. I thought Casey seemed nice, but how do we know? She could have been putting on an act for us."

"That's true. If Rayne died, it would solve three main problems. Richard would be free. He'd have a nice insurance settlement, and Casey would get the prime-time spot."

Hope replied, "Plus, they'd be able to marry too."

Kandi whistled. "That's a lot of motive."

Anne's phone rang. She picked it up and looked at the screen. "It's Richard."

Chapter Ten

After agreeing to meet with Richard later, Anne and Hope headed into Denver for breakfast at Snooze before heading to the botanical gardens. They wandered the paths, enjoying the beautiful display of various plants, but Hope noted her favorite was a display of all wildflowers. Finally, they left the park and headed back to Cherry Creek, where Richard had his apartment.

A disheveled Richard answered the door. "Come in." He motioned into the cool white marble hallway where large contemporary piece of art adorned the wall and a geometric sculpture sat near a doorway.

No English manor house style here.

Once they were inside, he moved past them into a large open plan living and dining area with a glimpse of a sleek, modern kitchen somewhat hidden behind minor wall partitions. "Please, have a seat."

Anne and Hope both took a seat on a gray leather sofa while he sat in a black and chrome chair next to the couch.

Hope broke the strained silence. "Richard, is there anything we can do for you or that you need?"

He shook his head, and Anne could tell he was struggling against breaking down. He blew out a breath before replying. "Thank you. I think it's finally hitting me. I'm trying to get it arranged in my mind, but I can't seem to function."

"Grief's like that. Especially when you love someone so much." Their eyes met.

"What gave me away?"

"Your face. Love was written all over it."

He rubbed his hands against his cheeks, bolting up from the chair. "I, yes, why shouldn't I admit it now? I love—loved—" His voice broke, and he took a moment to compose himself. "I did love Casey. But it wasn't mutual."

Anne's brow furrowed. "What?"

He returned to his seat. "I guess I should start at the beginning."

Hope reached over and laid her hand on his arm, signaling her empathy. "If you wouldn't mind, that would be helpful."

"We met at a gala event." He smiled at the remembrance. "She was funny, witty, delightful. Of course, beautiful as well. We connected right away."

"Did you meet Rayne then too?"

He shook his head. "No. I think maybe later in the evening, but we didn't speak. She was at another table for the event. I asked if I could call Casey, and she gave me her number. We went out, and things were progressing well. Then...it all seemed to fall apart. She wouldn't return my calls, ignored my texts. I couldn't find out what I'd done. Finally, I saw Rayne at another event. She told me Casey hadn't met someone else, but she didn't want to get into a serious relationship because her career was taking off. I thought that was the end of that, but then Rayne started texting me. Little things. How are you holding up? Want to meet for coffee, things like that. We started seeing each other. I didn't feel the same with her as I did with Casey, but she was so attentive, and it was nice to have someone who listened and appreciated the work I'm trying to do."

Anne stole a glance at Hope as if they could read each other's minds. Narcissistic personalities could easily manipulate you, and what better time than after a break-up?

"Over the months, we grew closer, and I thought I was falling in love with her. I felt so good when I was with her. Now I realize it was more to do with my bruised ego. One thing led to another. Then she called me, and everything changed."

"She told you she was pregnant."

"How did you—never mind—it doesn't matter."

Hope shifted to face him. "So, you decided to get married?"

He nodded. "Yes. They were doing a spot on vacations, and I went along with her. We were married on the beach. Just me and her. Witnesses were a few people who'd come along on the trip but no family. We planned to do a bigger church wedding with all the frills later."

Anne bit her lip, but she had to ask. "After your marriage, you took out insurance policies. I mean, that's what Rayne has said."

"Yes, if something were to happen to me, then I'd

want to ensure that our child was well provided for during their lifetime."

Anne caught that he didn't mention Rayne in his statement. "But Rayne also got a policy?"

"Yes, it just made sense for us both to get one. Married couples do." He stood up and paced the floor in front of the tall glass windows. "Sadly, I've had some losses in my investments. I've had to pull from my savings until things turn around. I know it will be fine, but it doesn't look good. To be honest, I'm worried they may think I had a hand in this. Or worse, arrest me."

"What? Why?"

"I don't know if you recall, but I said I needed to go back upstairs. When I went up there, my bottle of sleeping pills was gone."

Anne perched forward on the seat, "Did you lock your door when you left?"

"No. I don't think I locked it while I was there. It was only us four."

"Four?"

"Myself upstairs and then Rayne, Casey, and Ivy on the second floor."

Hope cut in. "When was the last time you saw the pills?"

He perched on a nearby table. "Let's see. I went up to bed and took a quick shower, then popped a couple of pills, and then went to sleep." He stared at them. "I don't want this to seem like I take them all the time. It's just that my mind doesn't want to shut off.

Casey said she would take them when she had an early morning shoot and couldn't get to sleep early enough."

Anne thought about what he said. Did Casey normally take sleeping pills? Could it have been an accident that she took too many? It lined up with some of their early theories.

"No. It was only if she had to go to sleep around dinner time. She had a shoot the next morning, which makes what happened not make sense."

Anne pocketed his statement in her mind. She wanted to get him back on track with the timeline. "So, you went back to the room and couldn't find the bottle?"

"I did. It had fallen under the bed."

"Then that should clear you."

He shook his head. "Unfortunately, no. The bottle was empty. Of course, my fingerprints were on it as well."

After talking for a bit more, Anne and Hope took their leave. As they drove back home, each spent time in their own thoughts, contemplating what Richard had divulged.

When Anne made it home, she greeted Mouser before checking her messages. Nothing from Carson. She went to his number but paused. What could she say? That she had cold feet and was worried about losing her independence? She set the phone on the table and rummaged through her fridge for a snack. It was a bit too early for dinner, but a piece of fruit would be good to assuage her hunger until then. Grabbing her phone, she made her way out to the front porch, where she spied Mr. Cole mowing his lawn. He saw her as she moved onto the porch, taking a moment to wave before returning to his efforts.

If only his wife were as friendly.

Anne took a bite of the crunchy, sweet apple as a familiar cruiser pulled up to the house next to the Coles'. She bolted from her position, watching as Carson exited his vehicle. He spied her but didn't raise his hand in greeting. Instead, he turned and went up to the door of the house Anne had visited yesterday.

What had happened? She wanted to rush over to see why they'd called Carson, but she'd have to wait until he came over. By the time he made his way out of the house, Anne was beside herself. Was it about Dean? Had he too met an untimely death? That would certainly complicate things.

A loud 'ach' escaped her lips as Carson slid behind the wheel of his car, did a three-point turn, and drove back down the street. It was beyond obvious that he was still upset and not speaking to her. Well, let him sulk. She could stay silent, too. She went inside, slamming the door behind her.

As the hours ticked by and the night shadows snuck farther up the road, she gave up staring at her phone. She called Kandi, who was with Stewart at a noisy restaurant. "We're waiting on a table. How'd it go?"

"I can tell you later, but it leaves us with more questions than answers. I know you're busy. Enjoy your time with Stewart."

She heard a familiar male voice. "Is that—"

Kandi said, "Gotta go. Love ya."

Anne stared at her phone. So, Kandi and Stewart were eating dinner with Carson. Why hadn't they invited her? Maybe it was someone else who sounded like Carson. No, she knew his voice. Maybe they'd gone there, and he was already there. That was most likely what had happened. Yet, her heart twinged a bit that he hadn't called her to go with him.

She had to see if it was Carson. She put in his number, but it went straight to voice mail.

A text came back.

An automatic message: Unavailable. In meeting. Will respond later.

So he *was* with Kandi and Stewart.

Fine, whatever. She made her way downstairs, where she cooked an omelet with the eggs Kandi supplied from her chickens. She toasted some French baguette slices, smearing them liberally with butter and topping them with sweet carrot cake confit. A gift from one guest who'd stayed at the Inn. The wine she'd uncorked was ready, and she poured the Chardonnay into her stemless wine goblet. Finally, she lit a candle on the table.

"I can enjoy my own company, thank you very much." She raised the goblet. "To me. I'm awesome."

She took a sip and enjoyed the sweetness of the wine hitting her tongue. Mouser watched her from his perch across the room as she took a bite of the cheesy omelet, getting mushroom, onion, and pepper in that bite. "Um, yum. So good. Sorry, Mouser, but not sharing."

At that announcement, he turned in a few circles, and tucked his head to his chest, nodding off.

The crunch of the toast delighted her with its buttery and sweet flavors that complemented the savory omelet. Her mind wandered over the last days. The events at the Inn. The curiosity of the actor across the street. Richard's speech to them today.

If he thought people were pointing the finger at him, he'd want to get out in front of it and share his side of the story. That's what had happened as their visit with him had wound down, and he'd revealed the most important of the information.

Anne recounted his words.

"I thought I could go through with it. It was like I'd been in a fog and suddenly it lifted. I realized the marriage had been a mistake from day one. We were still living separate lives. I went to Rayne and told her I wanted out. That I'd ensure our child was cared for. I even said I'd commit to a reasonable amount of alimony if she wanted it.

"Funny thing, I think she was more worried about her reputation than anything else. She didn't say anything about the baby, or us, or me. No tears. Nothing. She said she'd let me know. That's when she came up with this scheme. Big pretend wedding would garner lots of publicity, and then afterwards, it would be leaked that I'd been cheating on her. She'd gain the sympathy card."

Anne remembered the scowl on his face as he recounted the events.

He'd continued, "Rayne is always about ratings. Hers have been dropping. I think she may have heard about the good response from viewers when Casey stepped into her shoes when she was away with me. It had upset her to the point where she'd thrown things. I'd never seen her like that before. That's when I knew it would never work between us. We were two different people."

There was no mistaking that Richard had painted Rayne in an extremely bad light. So who was telling the truth—him or Rayne? Casey had said some similar things, but she was also gunning for Rayne's job. Plus, she and Richard had dated before he started up with Rayne. Maybe they'd planned it all along together and something had gone wrong. Either Richard had put the pills in the wrong glass and Casey had drunk it instead of Rayne, or Casey had done it and maybe forgotten that the glass had been doctored.

Plus, it was convenient that both Dean and Ivy had left almost immediately after everything happened. Anne needed some answers. Two were suspects and one was dead. Then she remembered. She could get in touch with the cameraman, Lee. Maybe he could give her some information. The thing about being the cameraman is that no one ever paid attention to you much. That gave you a front-row seat to things that occurred while others weren't on guard.

Anne looked at her now empty plate, devoid of the meal she'd eaten without even realizing it. She picked up her dishes and rinsed them off before putting them in the dishwasher. Setting Mouser's morning feed tray, she checked that the back door was locked before heading up to bed.

Tomorrow everything would be better and clearer. But for now, she needed a break.

After getting in her pjs, she clicked on the television. The news was on, and there was a picture of the Brandywine Inn. She scooted forward on the bed.

The shot panned to her speaking about the Inn, a few shots of the interior and exterior, and then Rayne spoke while a picture of Anne and her ex-husband appeared on the screen. Anne felt like she'd been punched in the gut. Rayne went on about her and Duke, about her tragic life, and so much more. To have it plastered across the screen once more made her cry out. Rayne had gone after her, her reputation and that of the Inn.

Anger bubbled up in her. Richard had been right. Rayne had done it for the ratings. When would she be free from her past? She gathered up a pillow and screamed into it. There was only one question in Anne's mind.

Had Rayne simply done her job as a journalist, or was this something else entirely?

Chapter Eleven

Anne thought about calling the station and asking to speak to Lee, but she knew you received a lot more information if you could see someone's face. Plus, she wanted to have a chat with Rayne. She'd fumed all night about it but decided in the end that it would be better to bide her time. She'd already ignored calls to her phone and text messages that had poured in. Knowing it wouldn't be long before reporters showed up, she posted a simple piece of white paper with the words: NO COMMENT in bold, black lettering and affixed it to her front door.

She stopped at the local gas station and filled up her tank. As she stood waiting for the pump to click off, she texted Carson: Come over tonight?

She'd realized it was foolish not to at least try, so was delighted when she heard the ping of a message. That quickly changed when she looked at the reply: Can't. Busy.

Anger bloomed in her chest. What kind of game was Carson playing? Maybe it was time to admit defeat and give him back his ring. If he didn't love her enough to be available for her...oh, so that was it.

She pulled the pump handle from the car and set it back in its cradle before twisting the cap back on and slamming the door shut. Inside, she struggled with the seatbelt, pulling it forward and backward, until she screamed out in frustration. "Ugh, work, you stupid piece—" Tears sprang to her eyes.

Where had they gone wrong? A nagging and gnawing forced its way into her conscious mind. Where did *I* go wrong?

She'd have to think about it later. Wiping her eyes with the back of her hand, she started the engine and drove out of the gas station. The trip back into Denver was uneventful, and soon, she was making her way to the station. Anne parked and made her way to the entrance, which was comprised of a solid gray door, a keypad, and a camera situated off to the side. Searching around, she found a call button. She pressed it, and a buzzer sounded.

"Hello. May I help you?" A woman's voice came through the adjacent speaker.

"Hi. I'm Anne Freemont. I'm here to see Lee, the cameraman."

"I'm not sure he's here. I can—"

Anne responded, "I also am here to speak to Rayne about a possible guest spot."

"Hmm, okay. Let me check. Wait there."

Where else am I going to wait?

In a short time, a buzzer sounded, and Anne heard the click of the lock. She opened the door and found herself inside a nondescript hallway with closed doors off to the side. Making her way down the hall, she came to a desk with a young woman wearing her blue hair up in a messy bun. She sported a nose ring, and her gaze was on the computer screen in front of her.

"Hello. I'm looking for Lee or Rayne."

She pointed with a nail sporting chipped polish.

Anne made her way down the hallway and saw another set of doors. Over one, a sign "On Air—Quiet" was dark. She doubted they'd be in there, so she moved past to a door that was open. Inside, Rayne was speaking on the phone. When she spied Anne, she held up a finger, signaling that she needed a minute. Anne nodded and looked around the room. It appeared to be a dressing area where a rack held a display of solid color sheath dresses in primary colors. No wonder they all looked the same.

On another wall, plaques of various journalistic or media awards, along with some shelves of clear trophies, were front and center. Many bore Rayne's name.

"Anne. Nice to see you. How can I help you?"

Anne shouldn't be shocked at Rayne's response. "I saw your reporting last night."

Rayne produced a closed smile, but it didn't reach her eyes, "No hard feelings, okay? Just doing my job as a journalist."

"Totally understand. I recognize why you did it." Better than saying you tried to surprise me with your attack.

"Good. Well, I'm glad that's all settled. Now, how can I help you? I don't have much time as I have an on-site shoot soon."

"First, before I forget, do you have Lee's phone number?"

Rayne picked up a brush and ran it through her long, blonde hair. "Ouch."

"You okay?"

"Yes, I recently had these stupid extensions put in and I don't think they were done correctly. Why do you need Lee's number?"

"I was hoping I could possibly get some stills of the Inn. For publicity use."

"Oh, um, I'm not sure, but if he took some with his other camera versus his video camera, they may be available."

"Great. I also wanted to see if you were still interested in a possible guest segment. I mean, with your current reporting, I'd think people would want to tune in even more to it. It could be great publicity for me and my books and ratings for your station." Anne made sure to refer to the station versus Rayne specifically.

Rayne smiled. "Totally agree. I think we could set it up for the next few weeks. We'll be running a feature on some of the wedding event—the dinner, at least."

"What's happening with Richard? Are you divorcing?"

Rayne wiggled her finger at Anne. "That's a bit nosy."

"Sorry. I only wondered."

"Well, he did try to kill me, so I doubt we have much of a future after that."

"Is it possible that it was Casey and not Richard?"

"Interesting. I've not thought of that. Though I

wouldn't have put it past her." She shrugged.

"You know, the day that you said you saw someone, who was it you saw in the dress?"

Rayne stared at Anne before answering. "I can't even recall now. It was my dress and long blonde hair. Maybe it was a ghost warning me or a vision."

Anne bit her cheek not to break out in laughter. *Sure, that was it.*

"Did you see your dress after that?"

Rayne answered, "No. By the time everything had calmed down and I went back to my dressing room, the dress was gone."

"Did you ask Ivy about it?"

"No, do you think she had something to do with its disappearance?"

"Absolutely not. I just wondered."

Rayne set the brush back down on the vanity. "It's all been so tragic. I'm not sure I want to talk about it anymore. What's done is done."

"Of course. Oh, was there a reason you asked Richard to stay the night at the Inn? He told me you'd asked him to stay there."

Rayne stood. "When did you talk to Richard?"

Anne had to think quickly. She didn't want to be caught in a lie, so better to tell the truth. "Recently. He's concerned that some things may point to his involvement."

"That's an understatement. He tried to kill me to collect the insurance. I hope they arrest him, and he rots in prison."

"You do plan on divorcing him, then?"

Rayne bristled. "I have a busy schedule. I'm glad we got this chance to chat about the guest segment. Now, I have to go. I'll have someone contact you, and we can set up a date for the screening."

She stood, signaling the conversation was over.

"Sounds good. Thanks for your time."

Rayne gave Anne a closed, tight smile before ushering her out of the room. As soon as Anne had made it back into the hallway, Rayne closed the door behind her.

I must have hit a nerve.

After leaving a message for Lee, she drove home, a new thought about the day's events in her head. She needed another convo with Hope and Kandi to get their ideas on it.

Anne pointed to the whiteboard where she'd erased the earlier information after taking a photo. "What do you think, Hope?"

"You're right. It's a pretty narrow window. If we look at the timeline, let's say Casey returned sometime between six or seven. That gives her time to go to the studio, clock in, and then say she's not feeling well and can't go on. She leaves and comes back."

Anne continued, "Then, once she's here, she puts on the wedding dress for whatever reason—"

Hope jumped in. "Wait. Maybe she had an idea to

'appear' to Rayne again while she was in bed asleep?"

"A possibility. It explains why she had the dress on." Anne replied.

Anne paced the room. "She puts on the dress and ends up drinking from the glass with the sleeping pills. Rayne is also sick. I don't know. Something doesn't seem right to me. If you're sick, why would you put on the dress, and was she the one who'd taken it?"

"Good points. Maybe she felt ill, but it made her melancholy. She wanted to get some sleep, so she took the sleeping pills but took too many, so she wasn't able to get out of the wedding dress before she fell into a coma.

Kandi came in from the bathroom where she'd been taking care of the ducks.

Anne said, "Kandi, do you remember what time it was when Ivy arrived?"

"Um, maybe nine? I was so busy with prep, I didn't, like, pay attention."

"Me either." Anne walked to the board. "Let's say we have a two to three-hour window between when Casey came back and when she was found barely alive. Listen, if you were sick, would you take sleeping pills?"

Hope said, "I wouldn't. A nice cup of valerian tea is my go-to. But it seems a bit weird. So, let's go with our other premise. She meant to give the pills to Rayne but got sick, forgot she'd put the pills in the water, and drank it. By the time she remembered, she rushed back to the dressing room, but it was too late."

"Certainly a possibility. But Richard said the pills

in his prescription bottle were missing. Did she know he was staying at the Inn, go upstairs and take the pills, then come back downstairs, put on the wedding dress, and then—I don't know." Anne sighed as she leaned against the desk. "I just don't get the point of putting on the wedding dress."

Kandi jolted up from her spot. "What if she was the one who'd spooked Rayne, and she meant to do it again?"

"We were just discussing that when you came in. She knows everyone will be asleep. She puts on the dress, meaning to scare Rayne, who'd be asleep. All she'd need to do is stand by the door to her room— just enough for Rayne to wake up and see her, then rush back to bed. Everyone would think she was still at the studio."

"Let's run with that for a minute. So, she gets dressed, but Rayne isn't confronted. Which means, one, it didn't happen as Rayne would have said she'd seen something, or two, Rayne wasn't in her bed, which could be the case if Rayne was already sick and was in the bathroom," Hope said.

"That makes sense. Let's say she, like, goes back to her room, thinking she'll try again. She waits a bit, comes back, and maybe she, like, hears someone or something which causes her to go into the dressing room next door. While she waits, she sees a glass of water and drinks it, not realizing it's been tampered with."

Kandi acted it out with Anne and Hope chuckling

as she skulked across the room, glancing over her shoulder and drinking from an invisible glass before falling dramatically into a vacant chair.

Anne responded, "Which then points the finger back to Richard. I'm thinking that he may have killed the wrong woman accidentally."

Hope said, "Okay, let's explore that. He agrees to stay at the house. He thinks Casey is in Denver. He goes downstairs and doctors the glass. Because it's in the dressing room, it would be a while before Rayne came in to drink in, thus having more people around in the morning and more suspects."

"I don't know. Wouldn't it cause sediment at the bottom of the glass if it sat too long?" Anne asked.

Hope nodded. "Hmm, yeah, I think you're right."

"Where does that, like, leave us?"

Hope sighed. "Still stuck, I'm afraid. I don't know if we'll ever be able to solve this. I do know that it is causing us the wrong kind of publicity for the Inn. We have to talk about its future."

"Speaking of, like, the future, Stewart popped the question last night."

"What?" Anne and Hope cried.

Anne said, "Kandi, that's wonderful. Please tell me you said yes."

Kandi's head bobbed, and a huge grin broke over her face. "I did. I'm so happy!" She squealed.

"We are too. That's wonderful," Hope chimed in.

Anne stilled. "Wait, last night?"

"Yes."

"When you were with Carson?"

"No. He just came in to pick up an order to-go. He saw us and thanked Stewart for the all the help with the lighting."

"Oh, okay."

Anne looked at Kandi's hands. No ring. Though younger people tended to do more of the silicone ring versus diamond or gem engagement rings, she'd noticed.

"Well, we need to have a party to celebrate. Too bad we got rid of all that food."

Kandi shrugged, "To be honest, I kept meaning to do it but haven't made time yet."

"We still have the cake and everything?"

"Yes," Kandi replied sheepishly. "I took the perishable stuff over, but I haven't had a chance to take any of the other items."

"Well, this is one instance where your procrastination may have benefited you."

"I feel bad, though, about the nonprofits. Maybe instead of gifts to us, people could donate?"

"That's a wonderful idea. Plus, then the nonprofit could use the money wherever the people needed more help."

"If it's okay with you all, I'd like to have the wedding right here. It's already decorated, we have the food. What do you think?"

Hope responded, "I think it's a wonderful idea. No matter what happens with the Inn in the future, we need something good to occur here. The sooner the better."

After they hugged, they left to go home, and Anne texted Carson: Have you heard the good news about Stewart and Kandi? Please call me when you get a chance.

The hours ticked by, and finally, Anne gave up, getting ready for bed. But that night, her sleep was troubled. She tossed and turned and woke with images flashing through her mind.

Flashing.

Wait.

She had left her bedroom door open, and she walked across the landing to look out the window and see flashing lights on a deputy's cruiser at the rental house.

"What in the world?"

In a moment, she watched as the young man who had been playing the game was escorted out of the house with his arms behind his back in handcuffs. She'd have to ask Carson about that as well. As they drove away, she looked across the street to the Coles'. The curtain dropped back into place. One of the Coles, and Anne was pretty sure of which one, had been watching what was going on. It gave her an idea.

Tomorrow, she'd be visiting the Coles.

Chapter Twelve

Anne took a deep breath and opened the door.

She wanted to launch herself into Carson's arms, but she held herself back due to the look on his face.

"Come in." She opened the door.

"For a minute." He walked past her, and it took everything not to reach out and touch him.

He removed his Stetson and wiped his brow. "What it is?"

While she wanted to ask about the events of last night across the street, she didn't want to cause more problems. "I think we need to clear the air between us."

"Okay." His rigid stance didn't relax.

She swallowed. "I, well, I, think we said things we didn't mean the other night."

"You're wrong. I meant everything I said. You have a decision to make. I love you, but I'm not playing games anymore. You either want to marry me and for us to build our lives together, or you don't. It's that simple."

"I don't think it is."

"Well, you're wrong. I've been patient." He pulled a slip of paper out of his pocket. "You meet me at this address on Monday at ten or, well..."

Their eyes met. He wouldn't say the words, but she knew it would mean goodbye. He turned and walked out of the house, leaving her staring after him. Shaking, she sat down, her mind warring with her heart.

She spent the next few hours digging in the garden, the sun beating down on her. Tears dropped onto the earth as she contemplated her life without Carson. She grabbed hold of a mallow and pulled. Its deep root refused to budge. She yanked with both hands, causing her to fall back.

As she stared into the clouds, four words echoed in her mind.

What should I do? What should I do?

Having finished her gardening chores, Anne gathered the flowers she'd picked to arrange into a bouquet for Mrs. Cole. She set the vase down and decided to take a shower before heading across the street.

As she came out of the house, she noticed Kandi holding a box. "What are you doing?"

"Finishing up getting rid of all the duck stuff. You know, getting all my ducks in a row." She laughed, and Anne laughed with her.

"Have you spoken with Stewart about the date of your wedding?"

"We're thinking next Saturday. It should give us enough time for his mom and dad to fly in and for us to get the word out to our friends."

"That's awesome."

Kandi cocked her head. "You okay?"

Anne nodded, denying the knot in her throat. "Yep. Just been working in the yard today and a bit tired now."

"Well, you definitely got some sun. You should have worn a bigger hat."

Anne chuckled. "Don't I know it. I always think I'll just go out there for a few minutes, and the next thing I know, it's been hours. I'll slather more lotion on it tonight before I go to bed."

Kandi said, "Oh, I forgot to tell you. Stanley's going to walk me down the aisle."

"That's wonderful. I bet that made his day."

She smiled. "He said he was over-the-moon. Welp, gotta get going. What's with the flowers?"

"I'm taking them to Mrs. Cole. A peace offering."

Kandi shifted the box. "That's nice."

Anne took a few steps before turning back to Kandi. "Do you know what happened last night at the rental house?"

"I heard they arrested a guy there, but not sure what it was about." Kandi shrugged.

"Okay, just wondering."

She crossed the street and after taking a deep breath, rang the Coles' doorbell.

Mr. Cole answered the door. "Hello, there."

"Hello, Mr. Cole. I wanted to give you and Mrs. Cole these flowers. I realize all the goings on in the last few days haven't been great for quiet around here."

He nodded and opened the screen door. "Come on in. Martha! It's the neighbor lady."

Geez. They didn't even know her name. What kind of neighbor was she that they didn't even know her name?

Martha Cole appeared wearing a full apron over a day dress. She spied the flowers.

"Here, Mrs. Cole. I wanted to bring you these. I want to apologize for all the noise and everything else for the last few days."

Mrs. Cole made a noise, and Anne wasn't sure if she was agreeing with Anne or disgusted. "Those are some beautiful flowers. No need to go buy flowers for us."

"Oh, no. These came from my back yard." Anne stopped. Would that make it seem worse than store bought or not as good of a gesture?

"Beautiful. I've never seen these over there."

"I have a cutting garden in the back for my annuals like this. You know, Colorado is so finicky. I have a raised bed specifically for flowers like this. If you'd like, I could help you plant some in your yard."

"You'd do that for us?"

"Of course. I'm a garden designer as well."

Martha tutted. "We don't need to hire no fancy designer."

"I'm sorry, that's not what I meant. I wouldn't charge you anything. I feel I've not been very good as a neighbor, and I'd like to make it up to you all."

Martha seemed satisfied with Anne's groveling as

she turned on her heel. "Come on, then."

Anne followed the woman back to a kitchen that looked frozen in time. While the house was Victorian, someone had updated the kitchen in the sixties, and it looked like it hadn't been changed since then. There was a Formica table with metal legs and matching chairs.

"Iced tea?"

"Yes, that would be lovely, thank you."

Anne sat in one of the chairs while Martha busied herself with putting ice into tall glasses. She poured the tea over the cubes, and the sound of cracking could be heard as the tea met the ice. "Mint?"

"Sure."

Martha pinched off some mint leaves from a nearby plant, plopping them into the glasses. Mr. Cole stood in the doorway and waited.

Anne took a sip of the cold brew. "This is delightful."

"Honey's the secret." She moved briskly to a covered plastic container that was exactly like the one Anne's mother used. It brought a wave of nostalgia over her. Martha opened it up and began slicing large pieces of Bundt cake. She set a plate in front of Anne with a fork before handing another plate and a glass of tea to her husband then shooing him off. "Now then, let's get down to it. What did you see last night?"

Anne almost choked on her piece of moist cake. Martha was a gossip. Even better to learn what she knew. "Do you mean about the neighbor being arrested?"

"Yes. You're dating that sheriff, aren't you? What's the scoop? I don't want this place turning into a hood."

"I can't tell you. I wish I knew, but Sheriff Carson can't share what happens on arrests."

Martha sighed. "Well, fiddlesticks. First, that one boy running around all over the place dressed up like a priest. Now this."

"So, you saw him running over to the Inn?"

Martha nodded. "I most certainly did. Young people. No respect these days."

Anne asked, "Do you know if he was over there on the day before the event—when everyone started coming for the dinner?"

"Oh, is that what all the hoity-toity were doing? No, can't say I did. I only saw him that night. But then, I haven't seen him since after he left carrying the outfit."

"Wait, so when he left, he had it with him?"

"Far as I could tell." She speared a piece of cake with her fork, and Anne took another bite.

"This is delicious."

"Family recipe." She preened at the praise.

"I wanted to let you know that we will be having another wedding—but it will be the last one at the Inn."

"You don't say." Martha pursed her lips.

"Yes, it's actually Kandi. Next door."

"Ah, what a sweet girl. She's always bringing us

eggs from her chickens or meals like last winter when I was feeling poorly. Oscar sure appreciated that. I did too. Is she marrying that fella, uh, what's his name again?"

"Stewart?"

"Yeah, that's it. Good lad. Not like that other fella. Never did take a shine to him. Another piece of cake?"

"I better not. But I know Kandi would be delighted if you and Mr. Cole came to the wedding. It's not totally set with the date, but we can let you know soon."

"That would be dandy, but we're not strangers now. You can call us Oscar and Martha."

"Great. And we can set up a time for me to figure out where to put the flowers if you'd like."

"That's mighty sweet of you, child."

Anne moved to rise, but a thought came to her mind. "Martha, can I ask you a question?"

"Certainly."

"Sometimes I can't sleep—"

Martha nodded. "Don't I know it. Some nights it's up and down."

"It's about the other night—"

Anne slept better than she had in days, waking to bright sunshine filtering through the curtains on her bedroom windows. Mouser came up to her, and she spent a moment stroking his fur as he purred at the attention. It was nice to wake up without having to rush to get ready.

Yawning, she stretched and turned, allowing her arms and legs to find the cooler sheet edges. When she'd enjoyed her time of stretching, she sat on the edge of the bed, where she spied a large glass of water she'd placed on the end table. She drank it down, and as the cool water slid down her throat, it was as if the fog in her mind cleared away. She made her way into the bathroom for her morning hygiene routine. After dressing in a chambray shift dress, she made her way downstairs and started up the coffeepot before looking for a writing pad and pen.

Sitting in a chair at the kitchen table, Anne made a list of things to do. First up was to call Lee. He'd been out of town for a few days' break but would be back today. His help would be vital. Next up was to contact Richard. She'd need to figure out a reason for calling him.

Next would be to email Rayne about the upcoming show.

The alarm on the coffeemaker sounded. Anne rose and poured herself a generous amount of coffee, topping it off with a dollop of cream before sitting back down at the table. She took a sip of the brew, allowing its warmth and caffeine to infiltrate her.

Anne drew a line down the center of the paper. She also had to think about her personal to-do's. While Kandi was most certainly up, she'd wait to call her and see what she could do to help with the wedding. Plus, she needed to let her know about the invite she'd given the Coles. She'd need to get a dress for the event as well. She could probably look for one at the shops around Cherry Creek. The main thing would be distracting Richard in order to do what she needed to do. That went across from Richard's name on the list.

Finally, she added the meeting with Carson to her list and underlined it twice with three question marks behind it.

A knock on the door stopped her thoughts. Kandi stood there, a big grin on her face, her hair recently colored to enhance her normal red. "Morning!" she chirped as Anne unlocked the door.

"You too. Coffee?"

"Nope. I wanted to stop by and talk about the wedding."

Anne heated up her coffee. "Shoot. I had it on my list to see what you want me to do."

"Nothing. I've got it all under control. I re-did some of the cake, too over-the-top for me, and I'll be adding fresh, edible flowers to it."

"Oh, that will be pretty."

Kandi smiled. "I thought so. I've spoken to Spencer and Molly, and they can both help out again with their friends for the dinner afterward."

"I want to pay for that."

"That's unnecessary."

Anne grasped Kandi's hand. "I know. I want to. I feel pretty useless here. I should do something."

"That's why I'm here partly. I was wondering if

you could, like, make two arrangements for the stands in the gazebo and if you think you have time, smaller low arrangements for the tables."

"I'll make time. Leave it to me."

"That's another thing. We're waiting for a few weeks. Stewart wants to finish up some construction jobs so we don't have anyone waiting on that and we can take a longer honeymoon. I went ahead and took the cake to the nonprofit as I don't think it can last that long."

"Even better. Oh, before I forget, I invited the Coles to ensure they're on the list. Hope that's okay."

"Of course, it is. They're both such sweeties."

"I really have been remiss in not getting to know them. I mean, I waved to them when I saw them but never really made much of an effort beyond that."

"It happens. There's been a lot going on since you moved here, that's for sure."

Anne laughed. "You can say that again. Listen, what about your dress? I was thinking of going to the shops in Denver. Plus, I need your help on something else. I figure we could knock both things out in one trip."

"Works for me. I'm free today. Want to go in a bit?"

"Let me see if I can get a hold of Richard."

Chapter Thirteen

Anne could set a time for later in the day with Richard, so before long, she and Kandi were on the road to Denver singing along to *Annie's Song*.

"His songs make me happy and sad at the same time!" Kandi said.

Anne nodded. "I know what you mean. I keep meaning to go to his memorial garden up in Aspen. Just don't have the time."

"No. Haven't *made* the time."

"Okay, Miss Obi Kandi Kanobi. You becoming a philosopher now?"

"No. I just realize that much of what we say we don't have time for is really that we're not making the time for it."

"You're right. I need to be better about that."

"Yep. Especially with you on death's door and all." She winked.

"Funny. Do you have an idea for what type of dress you want?"

"I'm thinking something with a steam punk theme."

Anne groaned, and Kandi burst out laughing.

"Why, you little minx."

"I'm not sure yet."

"You'll know it when you see it. Plus, it will help me to know how formal of a gown I should get."

Kandi hit her hand against the furry pink steering wheel. "I've got it. You pick out my dress, and I'll pick out yours."

"Oh, no. I don't think—"

"Don't you trust me?" Kandi gazed over at Anne.

"Yes, but not with picking out my dress."

"Come on. It'll be fun. Plus, it will help us see how much we really know each other and what we like."

Anne cleared her throat. "How about this? I'll let you pick out some and try them on, and you can try on what I pick, but if we decide none of them are right, we get to pick our own dress. Deal?" She stuck out her hand.

Kandi shook her hand. "Deal. Oh, this is going to be a blast."

"Or a disaster!" Anne laughed. One thing about Kandi—she always made the day lighter and brighter with her cheerful optimism. Anne knew what a blessing Kandi was to her life.

The next hours flew by as they oohed and aahed over the beautiful dresses. As promised, each picked out five options, and Kandi was the first to try hers on.

When she came out of the dressing room wearing the third dress, her eyes were sparkling and wet with unshed tears. "This is the one."

"Yes, you look beautiful. I knew you would. But don't start crying, or you'll have me crying too!" Anne wiped at her eyes.

"Okay, I'm going to try on the others just to be sure, but I think this is it."

Kandi ended up trying five more, along with a few that she selected but ended up with Anne's choice.

"Whew. That's hard work." Kandi slouched into the chair next to Anne. "Your turn."

Anne went into the adjacent dressing room and came out holding a wildly crazy dress. "Are you serious?"

"You promised!"

Anne finagled herself into the form-fitting dress with the low neckline. "Here. Happy?"

Kandi burst out laughing. "I wanted to see if you'd actually try it on! Is it the one?"

"If I could actually move, I'd hit you over the head." Anne returned to the dressing room and wiggled out of the dress. The next one was a simple shift of satin with a layering of ivory lace. She shook her head. Too much like a wedding dress. But she modeled it for Kandi, who remarked how great she looked in it. "You're not fully back in my good graces, but it's a start."

Back in the dressing room, Anne spied the next dress. A satin A-line in a soft peach topped by a bodice with cream lace cap sleeves while the skirt was covered in a lighter toned chiffon overlay, allowing the color to shimmer underneath.

Anne stared at herself in the mirror. Kandi had done it. She had picked out the perfect dress. As she opened the door and stepped out of the dressing room, Kandi exclaimed, "Oh, you're beautiful. It's perfect on you." Other women shopping nearby also gave their endorsements of the gown. "So, it's the one?"

Anne smiled. "It's the one."

Kandi stuck out her tongue. "See, told ya!"

After the dresses had been paid for and encased in garment bags, they left the store and made their way out to the truck.

"Do you think we should lay them on the seat or hang them? I'd hate for someone to steal my dress."

"With the truck locked and the back windows tinted, they should be fine. We need to get the shoes taken care of while we're here. Plus, I'm getting hungry. Let's grab a bite too."

A few hours later, the truck laden was down with new shoes and other bags, and the pair made their way over to Richard's apartment.

He greeted them at the door. Since the last time she'd seen him, he had improved in his appearance, if nothing else. He'd shaved, a recent cut near his chin attesting to the fact, and he'd had a haircut. He was dressed in khakis and a polo shirt, open at the neck.

"Do come in. I'm sorry I can't stay too long, but you said you had some news."

Anne nodded, but replied, "Oh, my gosh. I can't believe this. I'm sorry, but may I use your bathroom? We've been shopping all day—" She tilted her head in what she hoped looked like an earnest gesture.

"Be my guest. Third door on the left down the hallway."

Anne glanced over at Kandi, who was to create a diversion by having him point out landmarks in the city. As Kandi rattled on about the view, Anne slipped down the hallway. Thankfully, doors were open, and she spied his bedroom with a large king-size bed taking up most of the room and facing the plate-glass windows overlooking a view of downtown. She made her way into the bathroom, but it yielded no clues. The walk-in closet, smelling of musk, held suits, slacks, and an assortment of starched shirts. She opened the doors of the center island dresser, but nothing appeared.

Anne thought, *Where would you—*

She made her way back into the bedroom. The king-size bed was made up with a duvet and a bed skirt. Dropping to her knees, she lifted the bed skirt and peered into the dark cavity under the bed. At first she spied nothing, but just as she was about to give up, she looked toward the headboard.

It was balled up, but Anne knew what it was. She couldn't take it with her. For now, it was safe where it was. She made haste to head down the hall and into the guest bath, where she flushed the toilet. After turning on the sink, she came back into the living area, her hands rubbing together with the lotion that had been provided. "Thanks so much. Too much tea at lunch."

"No worries. Now you said you had news?"

"Did I? Oh, yes, um, I was wondering if there would be a funeral for Casey."

"Not here. Her parents came, and it will be back in her hometown somewhere up in Pennsylvania, I believe."

"Oh, right. Well, I wanted to let you know that Kandi and Stewart are getting married, and we'll love for you to come. This way, you'll have better memories about the Inn."

A confused look passed over his face. "I thought you were going to tell me something about what had happened with Casey. Some news there."

"Oh, sorry. I must not have made myself clear. But I will let you know something if we do. Now, we must go so we can beat the Denver traffic." She gave Kandi a look, and the young woman scurried toward her.

"Thanks for the information about the city. I bet it's simply beautiful at night. Oh, and hope you'll come to the wedding."

They waved goodbye and, outside of his door, hit the button for the elevator. "Come on, come on." Anne punched it a few times.

"Doing that isn't going to help anything."

"I know that. But it makes me feel better."

Once they made it down to the truck, Kandi turned to Anne. "Did you find it?"

"Yes, it was just what I thought."

"What should we do?"

"There's nothing we can do now." She glanced up at the block of apartments. Richard stood at the windows, looking down on them.

Later that night, Anne kept mulling over the incident. She wanted to tie this up, and soon. While Hope had agreed to let the people who'd reserved for the harvest fair in the fall stay on the books, they still needed to talk about opening it back up for the rest of the summer or even through the end of the year. Tourists were often eager to book rooms during that time, so they needed to decide soon as they had some on the books from last year.

Kandi had dropped Anne off at her house, and Anne took her time hanging her dress up where it wouldn't get crunched in her closet. Victorians weren't known for their huge closets, often requiring armoires or other chests of drawers for storing clothing.

Even though they'd had a substantial dinner with plenty of leftovers from the Factory, Anne was in the mood for some popcorn. She popped some and grabbed the butter from the fridge. After melting it, she drizzled it over the popcorn. Anne spied her note pad from earlier and glanced at it. What was she missing?

Maybe it was time to go back and look at the motive.

She printed out Casey. This one was more difficult because it still wasn't known if she had taken the pills accidentally or if she was given the pills on purpose.

Anne printed out another word—Assumptions. First, if Rayne was correct that she'd been the intended victim, the assumption would be that Casey took the pills accidentally.

Anne grabbed some of the popcorn kernels, popping them in her mouth and enjoying the butter and salt on the crunchy treat. She wiped her fingers on a nearby napkin before a thought came to her.

She wrote under the assumption column—glass in Rayne's dressing room. Had it always been there or placed there? If so, by whom? She wondered if she could get Deputy Ruiz to let her look at the photos they'd taken of the rooms. Oh, wait, she'd forgotten that she'd told Kandi to go take photos. She texted Kandi a note about uploading the photos so they could look them over.

Anne added another column with Rayne's name and a column for assumptions. Rayne said she'd been ill. Had she been given some pills through another medium but had luckily been sick, thus not causing her any harm? They only had her word that she'd been in the bathroom, ill, so had heard nothing in the room next door to hers. Under assumption, Anne wrote: Sleeping when Casey returned so didn't hear anything next door?

Then, of course, there was Richard. She added a column for him as well and under assumptions wrote: Asleep when everything was going on. Only have his word on that.

Anne thought back. It was his pills. He could have snuck downstairs and put the pills in the water container with no one seeing. He knew Casey would be away and Rayne sleeping. Then gone back up, took a couple of pills, headphones on, and off to sleep. Thus, appearing later with no idea what had happened.

She pinched some more popcorn in her fingers before popping it in her mouth, crunching down on it. What was missing? Or who?

Anne wrote Ivy as the next name. Under assumptions, she added: Only Ivy's word she received a text to go back to Rayne's apartment. She could have easily sent the text, as she had almost constant access to Rayne's phone. Maybe she already had the jewelry but knew Rayne would send her back to Denver for it. They assumed she'd left after everything happened, but what if Rayne had already given her the boot and told her she wasn't giving her a recommendation? She'd have to start over with another internship. That would be tough now unless she found something in the fall which could mess up her senior graduation schedule. Would that be worth killing for?

She tapped the paper with her pen. Geez, of course. It wasn't only those four. It was also the people who'd stayed at her house. Lee, the camera operator, and Candace, the producer, plus a few others.

Ugh, that would be another list of suspects to consider. Certainly, the Inn was locked at night, but they would have been given the key code for the back door so they could come and go as needed. While she had noticed nothing from Candace toward any of the newscasters, Lee's facial expressions at some points had made it clear he wasn't a huge fan of Rayne's.

Anne listed out the names Rayne, Richard, Ivy, Lee, and Candace, adding Casey at the top before circling the list.

One of them was a killer, and Anne was determined to find out who.

She sat back, staring at the names. Who gained from Rayne's death? She closed her eyes and took a deep breath, allowing her mind to wander. Snippets of conversations rose in her mind.

Who had anything to gain if Casey died?

If only the killer had made one mistake, it would be their downfall. Anne picked up her phone. She had work to do.

Chapter Fourteen

Anne arrived at the news station on Friday with Carson in tow. She'd explained everything to him and had asked for his help. Finally, he'd relented and made a call to his buddy on the Denver police force.

Inside, a small group of people were gathered around the reception desk. Candace walked over and shook Anne's hand. "Thanks for doing this. We'll shoot a longer segment today, and then we'll go back in and do the edits for the shorter televised versions." She waved a hand at a man standing nearby. "I believe you know Lee."

"Yes, hello, Lee."

He nodded.

Others would arrive after they'd gotten started, along with Kandi, who was excited about seeing a live taping.

They made their way into the taping area. A green screen was behind them, and Rayne entered from the side door. She beamed at the group. "Hello again, Anne. I'm so glad you decided to do this segment."

"It's a terrific opportunity. Plus, I've spoken to Candace. I had an idea that I think will really bring in the ratings. She's agreed to it. Especially coming off your last segment about me."

Rayne smiled, but there was a swift dropping of the happy face mask before she replied, "Wonderful.

Candace knows what works for us. Shall we?"

After a few minutes of positioning and some preliminary guidelines on where to look and how to show items on the table in front of them, they were ready to begin.

"Okay, don't worry if you mess up. We'll cut that part out. The main thing is to enjoy yourself."

"I will. Thanks," Anne replied.

A bit of music came on, and Rayne smiled into the camera. "We're here with Anne Freemont. As some of our viewers may recall, I did a feature on Anne a short while ago. Anne is the author of..."

Anne kept her mind focused as Rayne droned on about her books, the Inn, and the move to Carolan Springs. She glanced at a window and spied Carson and Kandi. Kandi made a "oh-my-gosh" face as she bounced up and down with enthusiasm. Farther back, Anne two other individuals stood in the shadows. She faced Rayne.

"Thanks for having me. As you noted, I've been an author, I do garden consulting, and lots more. You even alluded to my solving some crimes. I've always been one to enjoy fitting puzzles together. But to be honest, sometimes, it's something simple that gives a killer away."

"Oh, that's interesting." Rayne smiled for the camera.

"Yes, and it's often something someone says that triggers a thought. It niggles in my subconscious. Then another person will say something, not realizing its importance. It becomes another puzzle piece. I don't even realize this is going on in my brain."

"Fascinating. I bet it's like the way you plot out a garden or create your book." Rayne deftly moved the conversation back toward Anne's books.

"Yes, I loved writing the books and working in gardens. But you see, they have one thing in common."

"Ah, do tell?

"A plot. You outline a book, you plot the way a garden should grow, and it's also what happens with a murder. Of course, there're distinct types of murder as known by watching shows."

"We all love a good murder mystery. We have some good ones on our channel." Rayne spoke facing the camera.

"Yes, sometimes, the murder falls under the manslaughter category. As you know, my fiancé is a sheriff, and so I've learned about the diverse types of murder charges. He came with me to the studio today, in fact."

Rayne supplied a full smile of white teeth. "We'll have to be on our best behavior then."

Anne continued, "If you'll allow me, manslaughter is when a person is killed but without malice. In other words, the death could be unintentional. For instance, driving under the influence. A person doesn't plan to kill someone but by getting behind the wheel, someone who may be killed is due to them being in the commission of an unlawful act."

"I feel like we're getting a law school course here." She smiled back at the camera before turning to face Anne. She held up a hand to the camera, most likely a sign to stop filming or a place to edit. "Anne, we need to keep this lighthearted. So, less on the lecture and something that would be interesting to our viewers. Okay?"

Anne smiled. "Absolutely."

"Great." She dropped her hand.

Anne turned toward the camera. "Of course, we are all interested in the person who commits a pre-meditated murder. These killers are cunning, they feel that they have thought everything through, but in the end, what usually points the finger at them is that they're human. And we all know humans make mistakes." She faced Rayne, who stared at Anne.

"Go on."

"Take, for instance, the recent events we hosted at our inn for a couple. A man made an off-hand remark to me, and it didn't really mean anything at the time." Richard stepped from the shadows, and she turned to see Rayne stiffen. "And then my sweet friend, Kandi, said something about how she was trying to break a habit of saying *like* when she speaks. She's definitely gotten better but was having little success in totally stopping it. Even when she'd focused on it, later it would pop up again."

Rayne held up her hand again, but Anne noticed the red light on the camera remained on. This was all being taped. "I think we're getting way off base here.

Let's wrap this up. I think something fun or—"

"How about a cliff-hanger? Then it could go into the next portion of the show."

"Fine. But after that, let's switch over to some tips for the viewers."

"Happy to." Anne smiled.

Rayne dropped her hand. "That's remarkably interesting. So, it was simple things that were able to help you figure it out."

"Definitely. For instance, this is a fun little puzzle."

She faced the green screen, and Rayne turned with her. On the screen was the footage of the station's CCTV camera. A woman arrived, used her keycard, and then grabbed the door. "Do you recognize the woman on the screen?"

"Yes. I believe that's me, but I'm not sure what—"

"Next one, please," Anne replied. They turned back to face the screen. A woman appeared in the same dress, her hair a bit longer than the first woman's and also a few inches taller.

"Picture please." A shot that Anne had seen earlier showed the two women side-by-side, smiling for the camera. They were the same height in the photo and, with makeup, could have been sisters.

"This is you and Casey, am I correct?"

"Yes, I don't know—" Rayne fidgeted with her hands. She turned, and Anne watched as Rayne sought Richard. A look passed between them.

"Last one please."

Another shot of the back door camera appeared. In it, a woman put in her keycard and entered the building.

Rayne looked at Anne. "That looks like Casey going into the building."

"You'd think that, at a glance, wouldn't you? But look at these side by side. Notice the first one, the second one, and the third one. The first and the third one match in height."

"That doesn't mean anything. A change of shoes could change the height."

"You're right, and I kept watching to figure out how to determine the truth. Because I knew there had to be something that would reveal it."

Rayne's face bore a smug look. "Oh, well. Sometimes, even good detectives can make mistakes."

"True. I kept focusing on the height, but then it came back to me about how we can't help but revert to our old habits. Especially when we're focused on something else."

Rayne's brow wrinkled. She turned back to the pictures, her eyes searching. When she turned back to the camera, she chuckled, before stating, "And that's all for now. I'm Rayne—"

"Oh, I'm not finished yet."

Rayne faced Anne. "I think you are."

"No. Let's watch the tapes again. Roll the tapes."

Anne watched as the first shots showed Rayne putting in her keycard, then entering the building, the next one showed Casey putting in her keycard and also entering the building, then it showed the last clip, and it froze as the woman put her keycard into the slot.

"Your error was that you forgot she was left-handed. You'd taken the wrong shoes with you but figured if anyone looked at the tapes, you could explain it away like you did just now. But habits are hard. Especially when it comes to our dominant hand. You used your right hand with the keycard and opened the door with your left hand while Kasey always used her left to use the keycard and open the door."

Rayne glanced toward the booth where faces stared at her. She wet her lips. "This is silly. There's no way that—"

"There's more than this. Why did you do it? Because you felt threatened by her, or because Richard loved her? You wanted to frame Richard, thus giving you even more publicity and sympathy."

Rayne's body shook. "I'm not saying anything else until my lawyer gets here. I want to leave now." She made her way to the door, only to be met by two female police officers.

She screamed, "Lee! Get the camera. This is a false arrest. This isn't right. I didn't do anything wrong. I'm being framed. "

Silence ensued after Rayne was escorted out. Anne looked at the camera. "And that's how you catch a killer!"

After a few moments of speaking with Jodie and Lee, they met up with Richard out in the parking lot.

He ran his hand down his arms. "I can't believe

she did that. Poor Casey."

"The worst part is that she spent a lot of time planning it. She thought she'd created the perfect murder, but she didn't consider two important things."

"What's that?"

"Other people and details. As they say, the devil's in the details."

"What about the baby, or am I right in thinking there was never a child?"

Anne nodded. "No child. It was a ruse to get to you. I imagine Casey had said something in passing about you being a gentleman and old school. All she needed was to get you a drink, have a wild weekend, and take it from there, playing up to your honor."

"Well, I was a fool because it worked." He sighed.

"What will you, like, do now?" Kandi asked.

"I'll have to stay here for a while, then I'll probably pull up stakes and head home. I think I've had enough of the States for a while."

"I hope you won't hold this against all of us."

He shook his head. "No, but I think it will be good to head home to do some healing."

Anne placed her hand on his arm. "Just so you know, when you get home, there may be some police at your apartment."

He bristled. "Whatever for?"

"Rayne had some help. She hired an actor who was told he was taking part in a murder mystery weekend. He dressed as a priest—"

"Oh, that young man, the night of the dinner?"

"Yes. He held a zoom call, and the police got more information from him. He's flying home next Sunday to give a formal statement. But he was given only as needed instructions from either Rayne or Ivy through texts. After Casey was found alive, Rayne had to act fast. If Casey came out of her coma, she would most likely point to Rayne."

Richard spoke, "But Casey died in the hospital. She didn't die from the sleeping pills."

Anne responded, "I went to see Casey. I saw someone getting into the elevator. I wasn't sure if it was you or the priest. Then I realized that you both looked alike at a glance. That's probably why Rayne picked him. Anyway, after he went to the hospital, we headed to your apartment. Rayne had instructed him to take his costume and put it under your bed."

"What? You were snooping in my apartment?"

Anne shrugged her shoulders. "Only to see if I could find the outfit. Most people don't look under their bed until possibly spring cleaning, and it was in a place where, even if the maid vacuumed, it wouldn't be found."

"Righty then. Though we still don't know what happened to Casey."

"Yes. I do. Right before I arrived, a woman in a nurse's uniform came out of Casey's room. She ignored me when I spoke to her and turned away quickly. At the time, it didn't register, but I had noticed that she was holding a syringe. She stuck it in her pocket.

"So? Nurses do injections all the time."

"Yes, but first they wear gloves, and second, they would have disposed of the syringe in the medical waste container either in the room or on a cart. She had no cart with her. And when I went in, Casey was still alive. I can't be sure, but I believe Rayne injected an air bubble into Casey's IV. She didn't know if it would work, but Casey was already in a weakened state. In some ways, it could have saved someone else's life."

"Whose?"

"Ivy's."

Chapter Fifteen

"Ivy!" Kandi shouted, causing heads to turn.

"Yes, I believe Rayne was getting worried about Ivy putting two and two together. You remember that Ivy was her assistant. So doing a lot of her errands. Rayne had to get her nurse outfit and black wig from somewhere. Remember Dean, um, sorry, the priest was working out of a theater company in Denver. He said he gave the outfit to a young woman. I'll bet that was Ivy. Of course, he wouldn't think anything of it, just thinking that she would be using it for the murder mystery weekend. And in fact, Rayne never contacted him directly. She did it through Ivy's phone or email. That's why she was upset when he came up to her at the dinner. She didn't want anything to tie back to her. It's also why she let Ivy go. She'd be gone before she started asking too many questions about that night.

Richard's phone beeped. "I've been notified that the police are arriving soon. I best be going now."

Anne reached out her hand. "I wish you all the best. I imagine our paths may cross again, but if not, it was nice meeting you."

"It was lovely to meet you as well, though I would have preferred better circumstances."

Carson had joined the group outside. He looked at his watch. "Ready to head home?"

"Yes."

"You did good in there, N.D. I do believe that justice will be served for Casey."

Kandi pouted. "I'm still confused."

"How about this? We'll order in—say pizza, and we can go through everything."

"Awesome. I'll call Hope on the way home. I know she'll want to hear it too."

"Great."

Anne took Carson's hand as they made their way to their vehicle.

"Who want's veggie, and who wants pepperoni?" Anne held up two plates with pizza on them.

"I'll take the veggie one!" Kandi replied.

After everyone had acquired a piece of pizza and their preferred cold beverage, they chatted about the upcoming wedding.

Kandi grinned. "We really want you both to stand by us as we say our vows."

"I'd be honored." Carson took Stewart's hand in his own while Anne and Kandi embraced.

"What about music?"

"We hired a DJ for the night. He'll play at the wedding, some softer music for the dinner, and then more fun music for afterward for dancing."

"Oh, boy. I bet the Coles will like that." Anne winked.

"I'm planning to put down a temporary floor for

the dancing. Then we can take it up after it's over. Are you all okay with that?" Stewart's question was directed to Hope.

"Sure. I don't see it being a problem. The main thing is to put some lighting or reflective tape or something in case there's a lip where someone could stumble or fall."

"Good point. I'll make sure I do that."

Everyone took their plates to the dishwasher. Carson nodded to Anne. "Okay, you have the floor. What's your version of events?"

"Well, first, we were approached about hosting the wedding. Then once they arrive, I—and some of you as well—are informed that the couple is already married." Heads nodded.

"I was also made privy to the fact that Rayne was pregnant. I think now that this so-called "leak" of information was on purpose. But before I go into that, let's look at the motive.

"Rayne knew Casey was being praised as a new lead. When Rayne had been away, polls had suggested viewers liked the combination with Casey and Brandon over her spot with him. So, job replacement is one motive. Second, even though their looks are similar, Casey is—was—seven to ten years younger than Rayne."

She paused at the thought. The poor woman had her whole life in front of her. If nothing else, she deserved justice.

Anne continued, "From talking with Lee, I

learned Rayne had her eye on Richard when she found out he owned an estate in the UK. She probably saw herself as some princess or something. What she didn't know at the time is that Richard is house poor."

"House poor?" Kandi chimed in.

"Yes, it's like when you have a big, beautiful home but can't afford it. It's not uncommon into today's world. Back in the old days, people received room and board along with a small stipend that allowed these enormous homes to stay in the black financially. They also had homes on the estate that were rented out and received some proceeds of any agricultural or ranching duties."

"Oh, like Downton Abbey!" Kandi squealed. "I love that show."

"Yes, sort of like that. Anyway, back to the story. Richard fell head-over-heels for Casey, but she didn't feel the same and was focused on her career. She didn't want to get into any major relationship. Or she could have stopped it moving forward if Richard had told Casey about his financial troubles and she had no desire to foot the bill. Estate or not. I'm not sure how Rayne worked her way in, but somehow, she caught Richard on the rebound. Then it was simple to state that she'd gotten pregnant over that short weekend. There are still gentlemen in this world, and he said he would marry her."

"Lots of moving parts, but it sounds plausible," Carson said.

Anne replied, "Yes. Also, I think she had already

been planting things in his mind about life insurance, so her tenacity paid off when they took out major life insurance policies. This way, she could go after both of them. Get rid of Casey and frame Richard for her murder by suggesting he tried to kill Rayne for the money."

Hope took a sip of iced tea before interjecting, "I agree she meant to get rid of Casey, but doesn't it make more sense to have lots of people around during that time? For instance, why send Ivy away? It could have gone badly, and the finger pointed at her."

"That's why the set-up was so important. What's the saying? Um, sometimes it's not what's there, it's what's missing? I now believe Rayne made up the entire story of seeing a dead body in the back yard. We have to ask why. I thought it was someone helping her to pull in ratings. You know marriage, haunted house, and so on."

"But all the time she was simply planting a seed," Hope said.

"Exactly. The seed she planted was that someone wanted her dead. Even if we didn't recognize it or believe she saw anything, it goes into our subconscious. We question who had played the trick on her or who hated her. It's manipulation at its finest."

Carson spoke. "Criminals are good at revealing the truth, even when lying. For instance, I had someone who noted he loved his brother, but the entire time, his head was moving from side to side, signaling no, I don't."

"Yes, even at the studio, you remember when Rayne said it looked like Casey, not that it was Casey. She knew it wasn't Casey."

"Go on. So, how did she do it?" Kandi said.

"Okay, so we go back to the night in question. I think she must have conned Casey into spending the night, knowing that she had an early set at the station. Remember when the van had been here but left. Casey could have easily done a spot from here, but the van left. So, Casey had to drive back into Denver because she didn't have anyone to film her. I'm sure at this point she was livid with Rayne."

"She confronted her?" Hope asked.

"I believe so. But it must have been after we'd left."

"But wouldn't Richard have heard?"

Anne shook her head. "No because he went out with Lee. Supposedly Rayne texted Lee about taking Richard out for a bit."

"Wait, so that means that the only two people in the house at the time were Rayne and Casey."

Anne pointed. "Exactly! Now I don't know what happened at that point, and I doubt we'll ever know, but Rayne invited Casey in for a drink. I think she shared how she was happy that Casey would be taking over for her."

"In other words, to massage her ego, thus causing her to let down her guard," Carson said.

"Exactly."

"But what about the dress?"

"I wondered about that too. But again, it all goes back to perception. Rayne said she 'saw' a dead body in her wedding dress. The only thing I can figure is that she asked Casey to try it on so she could see if the piece that had been cut from the dress was noticeable."

"But I thought the dress, like, vanished?"

"Yes, but what if Rayne had hidden it before she went outside? She told Casey she'd found it or something."

"Where were they at this point?" Hope asked.

"Hard to say. But I'm thinking that Rayne had brought glasses to Casey's room. To apologize. Act like she'd make it up to her. Then, after Casey was relaxed, she mentioned the dress. I think she may have put one of the sleeping pills in her glass or at least a half because she wanted her to be calm. After she took her over to the dressing room so they could look in the big mirror there, Casey may have realized she was unwell. Rayne pointed to the water glass that had the fatal dose of sleeping pills in it. Or to make it up to Casey, she'd promised to go in her place. Casey may have tried to move but ended up on the floor. Now that's where we don't know if Rayne's motive was to cause her to miss out on a segment or she really meant to kill her."

"Then she just left her? What a horrible woman!" Kandi exclaimed.

"Yes, she is. I think if you looked up psychopath in the dictionary, you would see her picture. She only cares for herself."

Hope nodded. "But that was a very short window after Casey came back."

"That's where Rayne made her mistake. She had to show that Casey had been alive during the night, thus giving her an alibi. She then took her place. But she didn't count on our neighbor who has trouble sleeping or making nightly trips to the bathroom. Mrs. Cole said that she saw the woman come out of the house. But she must not have wanted to unlock the car with her clicker in case it woke anyone. Mrs. Cole told me that she'd had trouble sleeping and had glanced out the front windows. At that point she didn't know who the woman was but as she was watching her, Rayne tried opening the wrong car door. She grew more frustrated when it wouldn't open."

"Ah, wrong car!"

"Yep. I've seen people do that all the time. It looks like yours, but it's not. Here, it was a different model. Rayne just knew it was a gray car. Finally, she had no choice but to click the unlock tab on her key fob, hoping any people hearing it would think it was Casey leaving. But now she was running late, and at some point on the drive, she realized she'd grabbed the wrong shoes. She knew it might be a problem but doubted anyone would notice. Which they wouldn't have if we wouldn't have put them side-by-side. The difference in height is evident, but she was so flustered or didn't think about it, that she made her biggest error."

"Using her right hand."

"That's right, Hope. Plus, I asked Mrs. Cole what hand the woman had held the key fob in, and it was also the right hand."

"But that makes sense, as the key is on the right," Kandi said.

"In most cases, yes. But Casey's car has an automatic start. Casey kept her key fob on her purse strap on the left-hand side. I remembered seeing it when she arrived."

"She wouldn't have been only carrying the key."

"Exactly."

"Anyone for dessert?" Kandi popped up from her spot and made her way over to the counter. Groans and "I'm too full" were replaced with "Maybe just one" as Kandi opened the container to show a variety of chocolate and peanut butter brownies.

Anne continued, "From his statement, the invite to go out with Lee was just a ruse to have a bit of a bachelor's party for Richard. He arrived back and, as far as we know, he went up to bed."

"Yes, his being gone allowed Rayne to get the pills she needed," Hope said.

"But I thought the bottle was almost empty. Or didn't he say it was, like, missing?"

"She could have taken some over a while or there was another bottle. I guess we won't know unless she reveals it, which I doubt."

Hope dusted chocolate crumbs off her hands onto her plate. "So, she left Casey there with Richard while she went into the studio?"

"You know, I didn't even think about it, but she could say she took Casey's place on purpose, thus pointing the finger back to Richard."

"Yes, but Casey didn't die from the pills. It was a shock to Rayne that she'd survived it. She had to do something because Casey would share what had happened, and the evidence would point back to her."

"So, what did she do?"

"She had Dean visit Casey on his way to the airport for his flight to Mexico. Once he left, she went in and finished the job. Most likely putting an air bubble in her IV or a vein. I told the police that they might find a nurse's outfit and wig at the theater where Dean works. It should have some of her DNA on it, and they'll be looking at the cameras around the hospital. She may have put on a disguise, but I doubt she changed cars."

"Poor Casey. She seemed really nice."

"Yes. I don't understand how people can hold such hate in their heart."

Carson squeezed Anne's hand. "That's a good thing. As much as you know I hate you getting involved, your work brought the killer to justice."

"Let's hope a jury thinks so."

Chapter Sixteen

Saturday dawned clear and bright as Anne listened to the sounds of a lawnmower next door. Spencer was cutting the grass this morning before the evening's festivities. The last few weeks had felt like a whirlwind with preparing the floral arrangements and ensuring the food was ready for the meal to follow the ceremony. Yesterday had been crazy with the time at the studio.

After partaking in some toast and a cup of coffee, Anne made her way over to Kandi's house, where they would have their hair and makeup done. As she walked out her front door with cup in hand, a silver Range Rover pulled up in front of the house next to the Coles'. A tall man exited the vehicle before going to the back and pulling out a For Sale sign, which he finagled into the ground before driving off.

That should make the Coles happy. At least if it was a family instead of another rental property. Looking around at the small cul-de-sac, Anne sighed with contentment. It was a beautiful area. She turned and faced her home. There were more decisions to make, but those could come later. She walked over to Kandi's house, where music blasted.

"Hello?" She walked into the entryway.

"Come on back!" Kandi yelled over the din of pop music.

Anne went in to find Kandi dancing around the kitchen with a few other familiar faces. Polly was there and looked to be dancing with one of Kandi's ducks. "I thought you were getting rid of the ducks."

"They decided against them, so Polly's taking them after they get a bit bigger."

"Don't you have a house full of animals, Polly?"

"Oh, I'm taking them to a farm over by Palisades. They're wanting them to keep the bugs down."

"Well, glad it's working out for them."

Polly smiled and placed the duck back down in a set-up constructed from a discarded refrigerator box.

Anne spoke to another pair of women. "You must be Kandi's friends from school. I recognize your faces from some pictures."

They nodded in unison. "So happy to be here for Kandi's big day. Wouldn't miss it for the world."

"That's awesome. Kandi, when do the hairdressers arrive?"

"I think around lunch. I figured we could eat a late brunch and then they'd have time to work on us."

"Sound good. I'm going to pop over and see how everything's going at the Inn. I heard the lawnmower, so that's taken care of. I'm going to set the floors in the kitchen there, and I'll have the kids put them out before guests start arriving. Are my eyes deceiving me, or do we still have the red carpets from Rayne's event?"

"Nope. They are letting me use them because they've gotten so much publicity after I shared their information when I was talking to the film crew. They said they were already getting lots of calls."

"Smart cookie." Anne winked.

"Actually, I wish I would have thought of it. I only said I was talking to them when the group started arriving. But I'll take it."

Anne hugged Kandi. "Okay, let me go make sure of everything, and I'll meet you all back here for brunch. Please tell me you have help for this and you're not doing it yourself?"

"I have to keep busy. I made the quiches last night and ordered in some other items. Molly is helping set it up."

"Okay. I'll be back soon." Anne made her way through the yard over to the inn that was bustling with people. Kandi had called in a caterer to help with the dinner. After everything that had happened, they'd decided to skip the original cake and give it away as well. Didn't want any bad memory to mar the day. The caterer had supplied three new smaller cakes. One chocolate, one decorated with various construction tools. The other cake was decorated with red icing and red candies. These two would sit on either side of a larger cake as the centerpiece. Anne didn't know why they needed three cakes, but who was she to question Kandi's choices?

After finding that she was more in the way than helpful, she made her way home, where she indulged in a luxury bath with lavender. She dressed in her new silk lingerie she'd bought on her outing with Kandi and covered it with a shift that buttoned in the front to be easy to remove and not mess up her hair in the process.

She'd already taken her shoes and gown over the evening before, so all that was left was one item. Anne picked up two boxes with red ribbons on them and made her way over to Kandi's.

Thankfully, the atmosphere was quieter when she arrived, and Anne could smell the savory aroma of the quiches. She set the boxes down behind a lamp before joining the others. A mimosa was thrust into her hand as she thanked the young woman who'd handed it to her.

Hope had arrived and was already dressed in a beautiful emerald dress that flattered her height and willowy frame. Her hair had been curled in order to provide height for her bob, and one side was held back with a beautiful rhinestone feather. Her ears were adorned with simple emerald studs.

"Hope, you look stunning. Where have you been hiding this gorgeous part of yourself? Seriously, you look like a model."

Hope leaned closer to Anne. "I had professional help."

"Oh, is Eliza here?"

"She'll be at the wedding. When I told her about it, she practically begged me to let her pick out my dress—oh wait, what did she say? 'Please allow me to supply your costume for the event.'"

Anne could envision the tall Ethiopian model with

her posh accent speaking to Hope. "Well, she has done it. How do you feel?"

"I'm fairly surprised. I feel a bit like Cinderella. It's not that I don't enjoy dressing up or fashion, but over the years, between my work and Mom, it's been the last thing on my mind."

"Well, watch out because I think there are going to be lots of moths drawn to your flame."

Hope laughed. "I'm still me. But I think Eliza's bringing a guest tonight."

"Great. Looking forward to meeting them. Here's to a wonderful day." She clinked her glass with Hope's. "Food?"

"No. I already ate. Plus, I need to go warm up."

"Warm up?"

"Yes. I volunteered to sing a song at the wedding."

Anne's mouth dropped. "I didn't know you could sing."

"I don't do it often, but this is a special occasion, so I told Kandi I would. Just this once."

"What are you singing?"

"*The Only One.*"

"Oh, I don't know if I've heard that one. Looking forward to hearing you sing."

"Thanks. A bit nervous, but I'll have music accompaniment from the DJ as a backdrop, so that helps. That's why I'm here a bit early. After the DJ sets up, we're going to do some practice runs for sound and timing."

"When are you singing?"

Hope smiled. "For their first dance."

"Oh, wonderful. Okay to hug you and wish you good luck, or is it break a leg?"

"I'll take whatever."

They embraced.

"I'm going to see if he's arrived. Enjoy your brunch," Hope said.

The ladies chatted and giggled as they made their way through the delightful brunch spread and bottomless mimosas. They had finished when the hairdresser and makeup artist arrived.

The time flew by as the women worked and chatted. Hope rejoined them and relented to a bit of a makeup touchup.

Anne picked up the boxes before she went upstairs and put on her gown. As she stood in front of the mirror, Kandi knocked on the door. "Come in."

"Whoa. You look out of this world."

Anne twirled in front of the mirror. "I doubt I would have even picked this dress, but I have to admit it's perfect. Is the photographer here yet? I should be helping you get dressed. But first—"

Anne handed Kandi the box.

"What is it?"

"It's my gift to you."

Kandi cracked open the box to reveal a dainty pearl necklace.

"I didn't know if you had something borrowed yet."

Kandi's eyes filled with tears. "No. This is

wonderful."

"They were my mother's. I guess you could say they're something old too. May I?"

"Yes, please." Kandi's hair was done in a half up, half down style, and she lifted it away so Anne could secure the clasp around her neck. She touched the pearls. "They're perfect."

"Not quite. Here." She handed Kandi a smaller box. "These are for you."

Kandi unwrapped the small box. Inside were a pair of ruby and pearl earrings. She gasped. "Oh. This is so much better than what I'd picked to wear. Thank you." She wrapped her arms around Anne's neck.

"We better stop tearing up, or we'll have to go back and have our makeup re-done."

Kandi laughed. "They already said they'd do touchups right before we go out. Plus, they only use waterproof mascara."

"Okay, let's get you into that dress."

Once Kandi had her wedding dress on, Anne put in the earrings for her. They stood in front of the mirror, neither speaking. Finally, Kandi said, "I never thought I'd feel so happy. I love Stewart so much."

"I'd hope so if you're going to marry him!" Anne teased. "Now let me gather up this skirt and train so you don't fall over it."

They made their way into another room where the photographer had set up a basic backdrop. Most of the formal pictures would occur after the wedding, but these would be more informal shots. All the ladies mugged for the camera.

"All right, sweetie. I'll see you out there." Anne kissed her lightly on the cheek.

Kandi's friends would help arrange the train behind her.

Music was playing as Anne took her place just behind a barrier, fiddling with the flowers in her hand. She looked up to see Lee taping her. He'd agreed to videotape the wedding as his gift to Kandi and Stewart. She smiled and waited for her cue to start her walk down the aisle.

Another melody picked up, and Anne took her first step on the carpet. Along the rows of white chairs, she smiled at those she recognized, nodding at the Coles as she passed them and acknowledging Eliza, who was beautiful in a chartreuse affair that most likely cost a fortune. Sitting next to her was a tall, handsome man. Ah, that must be the guest Hope shared. Good for Eliza.

At the steps up to the gazebo stood Stewart, trying to hide his discomfort at being in a tuxedo while Carson stood next to him as best man. For a brief moment, their eyes met, and he mouthed, 'You're beautiful.'

Heat rose to her cheeks as she moved over to the left, leaving room for Kandi next to Stewart. The sound of trumpets filled the air as the wedding march announced Kandi's arrival. Everyone rose and Kandi, escorted by a beaming Stanley, in dress blues that still fit after many years spent closeted, began her walk down the aisle.

When they reached the group, Stanley kissed her hand before finding his seat next to his wife. Stewart took Kandi's hand, and they mounted the gazebo steps. The pastor moved toward them, and after they had taken their vows, the crowd broke out in riotous applause. Anne wiped a tear from her eye.

After being pronounced husband and wife, the pair made their way down the aisle. There, they stopped and turned back toward the gazebo.

Anne had been waiting for Carson to take her arm and follow behind the pair. Just then, the pastor moved to the edge of the gazebo.

"Ladies and gentlemen, this is probably one of the nicest days we've had in a long time. In fact, it's so nice that I wonder if anyone else would like to get married right now."

A murmur and flutter of soft laughter went through the crowd. People looked around and pointed at each other. Anne's gaze went to where Stewart stood alongside Kandi, who was bouncing up and down.

She turned back when she sensed Carson beside her. He held out his hand. "Ready?"

She placed her hand in his. "Yes. Yes, I'm ready."

Chapter Seventeen

Anne had known that Carson was serious when he had told her to meet him at the marriage license office. While she hadn't planned this, it was fairly evident by Kandi and Stewart's faces that they had been in on it. Lots of it made so much sense now. But it didn't matter. She loved Carson, and he loved her. There was no point in delaying.

She started as the pastor spoke. "Anne, would you like to say anything?"

"Well, believe or not, I haven't prepared anything."

The crowd laughed.

Anne waited a moment before saying, "I'll simply speak from my heart." She gazed into Carson's eyes. "I love you, and you continue to show me you love me. And that's not easy, as you know. I'm hard-headed, and want things my own way, and often act before I should. Which is why I need you in my life. I need a rock of stability. Arms to enfold me when the world frightens me. A hand to pull me back when I rush into another stupid idea. I'm yours for better or worse and everything in between."

Carson smiled at Anne and took her hand in his big, meaty one. "I knew you were the one the moment I saw you. You have fire in your eyes, and you stood up to me. Well, you tried to on those wobbly shoes."

Chuckles could be heard as some recalled Anne's welcome to Carolan Springs.

"But I knew you needed time, and so I gave it to you. Now we have the rest of our lives to drive each other crazy. I'm yours for better or worse and as the old saying goes, 'with all my worldly goods, I thee endow.' I love you, Anne."

The pastor read a passage of love, and then rings were presented. Not surprisingly, Carson had them in his pocket.

"I now pronounce you, husband, and wife!" Everyone cheered as Anne lifted her face to Carson's kiss.

The DJ struck up the music, and they made their way down the aisle to where Kandi and Stewart stood waiting.

"You!" Anne gathered Kandi in a hug. "This is supposed to be your big day. I feel like we've hijacked it."

"No. This is, like, the best day ever. How many can say they got married the same day as their mom?" She winked.

"Fine. But now I understand why you were so keen on me getting a proper dress versus a simple normal hemline for today."

They stood beside each other as people came up and hugged them while giving them good wishes. Soon, people were claiming seats around the tables set up around the yard. Dinner went smoothly, with everyone enjoying the wonderful meal. Then it was time for Kandi and Stewart's first dance. Hope took the microphone, and Anne smiled as the pair swayed to the music. But something kept niggling at her mind. What was it?

A hand on the small of her back startled her. "N.D., what is it?"

"I don't know. You know that old saying of being led up the garden path?"

"Yes. Already having regrets?"

She kissed him. "Not about us. That's the only smart thing I'll ever do. No. But I think I've made a terrible mistake. And if I'm right, I'll have to live with that forever." She looked up at Carson. "Do you trust me?"

"What a silly question. Of course, I do."

"Okay, then if I'm right, we need to get going. Right now! I can tell you what I'm thinking on the way."

He nodded, and Anne rushed over to where Kandi and Stewart stood speaking to another couple.

"Kandi, I love you. But I have to go. We'll be back later." She kissed Kandi's cheek.

Carson grabbed Anne's hand as they made their way to her vehicle. It was blocked in by other cars.

"Oh, no. Maybe we can borrow Kandi's truck?"

"It's blocked too. If only we had your cruiser."

An older male voice spoke from behind them. "What seems to be the problem?"

"Mr. Cole, we need to see who owns these cars, as we have to get to the airport right away."

He winked. "Can't wait to start the honeymoon, huh?"

"No, we have to stop someone from getting on a plane," Anne said. "If I'm right, then we don't have time to waste. And it may be too late."

"Oh, that's a fine kettle." He looked at the cars blocking the driveways. "Much easier if we take mine."

Anne made a face at Carson, who shrugged. Mr. Cole was already walking to his garage, so they followed him. Inside, a tarp covered a vehicle. Together with Carson, they pulled the heavy cover back to reveal a 1967 Shelby Mustang.

"Is this what I think it is?"

Mr. Cole nodded. "That she is. Let's just say when I retired from the job I had with them, I only asked for one thing. Now, we need to get moving. Sorry, but one of you will need to sit in the back, such as it is."

Anne climbed in, and Carson moved into the front passenger seat.

"Just one question for you. If I get stopped, you'll bail me out, right?"

Carson nodded.

"Then we're good. Buckle up!"

Driving through town, Anne wanted to yell, 'speed up,' but once they hit the interstate, it was like another person took over. Mr. Cole shifted so smoothly that the car didn't even jerk, but Anne could tell they were rapidly gaining speed. Carson was on the phone with the Denver authorities, and Anne kept calling Richard's mobile, but there was no response.

She glanced over Mr. Cole's shoulder to see they'd passed the hundred mark.

"Hold on!" Mr. Cole yelled as he shot across three lanes and in front of various cars, leaving them as spots behind them.

"Where did you learn to drive like this?"

"Between collaborating with a team to improve a car's performance, along with an undesired stint in 'Nam, let's just say I learned to drive fast."

"It's impressive," Carson responded.

"Ah, this is nothing. But I don't want to scare your missus in the back seat. She's already a bit green around the gills."

"Anne, honey, you okay back there?"

"A bit car-sick, but I'll be okay."

Carson's phone rang. He answered then nodded. "Will do."

Anne replied, "So?"

"They got the description you sent. They also narrowed it down to a few names. They'll meet us at the gate."

"No, most likely in the lounge. But hopefully before security and on down to the trains."

"Even better. Our presence will be an unwelcome surprise."

Mr. Cole shot to the curb as the police moved toward his car. Carson hopped out, showing his sheriff's badge and explaining how Mr. Cole had helped them get there. He then turned back and helped Anne from the car. "Feeling okay to make a bit of a dash for it?"

She took a deep breath and swallowed. "I've come this far." Hiking up her dress, she ran after Carson, their hands entwined. They made it to the concourse and looked down on the queue of people sneaking around the lines of the baggage check.

"There he is!" Anne pointed.

He was still far enough behind another group that they could make it downstairs. Carson motioned toward the police and the TSA agents who came running toward them.

Running from the escalator, a TSA agent pulled back the tape, and within a few minutes, they were taking the struggling person by both arms to the side where they stood waiting. They had barely made it. Anne searched the crowd but struggled to see her intended target.

She gasped. Rushing over, she looked into the face of a killer. "Hello, Dean."

"I'm sorry. You must be mistaking me for someone else, lady." Gone was the posh British accent, the chestnut brown hair, and the crisp white shirt and slacks. Instead, here was a man with shorter, blond hair with a buzz cut in jeans and a hoodie, carrying a simple backpack slung over his shoulder.

"Oh, would you prefer I call you Richard? Or how about your real name? That would be a good start."

Carson stood next to Anne, and Richard's gaze took in the advancing transportation agents and police.

"Huh. Well, what d 'ya know? So, what gave me away?"

"A couple of things. Rayne never faltered from her story that you were to blame. Even when presented with all the evidence. Plus, there were a few other things. I hadn't realized they were there all along until today."

"Enlighten me."

"First, Dean. It was no coincidence that he looked exactly like you. You hired him, not Rayne. That's why she became flustered when he tried to speak with her at the event. She didn't know him or know what he wanted. Then it was easy to get the real Dean out of the picture while you borrowed the priest's outfit and went up to visit Casey. You couldn't let her wake up, as she'd let them know you were the one who'd been there when she blacked out."

"Hmm. Could be. But what about Rayne going to the station imitating Casey? Pretty incriminating if you ask me."

"You made her feel bad about Casey. Somehow, you convinced her to take her place. Or she did it on her own. I'm not sure of that yet."

"I'd say you're not sure about anything."

"I'm quite sure you're the killer. And you certainly aren't British either."

He smirked but said nothing.

"I also wondered how you weren't upset over being tricked into a marriage. Something didn't sit right with me that you weren't at least a little angry over it. I doubt Rayne ever even said she was pregnant. You just used it and had her go along with it, too. Certainly, the station wouldn't want to let her go at that stage or they would look unsympathetic, or she could play the 'you got rid of me because I'm pregnant' card. You must be surprisingly good at manipulation."

He shrugged. "You know, sometimes people only need a push. They're already there themselves. You just have to give them a nudge. Rayne is no saint."

"It was you at the hospital. You didn't care about Casey, but you had to make it look like Rayne played a part in her death. That's why you hired the actress who looked similar to Rayne and had her go into Casey's room, where you then shared that she was no longer needed. That's why she wouldn't talk to me. She wasn't a real nurse and would get in trouble for being in the patient's room."

"Interesting. Go on."

"Two things. First, your apartment. It had no personal touches whatsoever. That's when I realized that it was most likely a rental. You didn't own it at all."

"I never said I did. Guilty. So what?"

"Possibly. But you implied it was yours. Just as you took on the name of Richard and his estate in England. It would be enough that if Rayne looked, you would seem legit. But Casey saw through your ruse right away."

"Tell me. Why would I try to kill Rayne or Casey? I gain nothing from Casey's death."

"That stumped me for a while. Then it came to me.

It's simple. Money. My guess is you go after women around the world, inventing personas to suit them. You went to the gala, posing as Richard. After Casey rejected you, you simply moved over to Rayne. Casey didn't have the money you needed. I'm curious, though, how did you get Rayne to take Casey's place that night, further implicating her in Casey's death?"

"Well, I'm not sure I can say. But if I had done something like that, I'd have played on her vanity, saying something to the effect of there being consequences for not showing up for work and not calling. Then let's say that she decided to get someone drunk and put a few sleeping pills in a glass. And then let's say that someone else came along and added some more. But that's just conjecture, of course."

"That still doesn't answer the question."

"Funny but turns out Rayne felt bad about doing what she'd done. The woman has a heart after all. She found me and asked what she should do. I may have given her some ideas, and Rayne decided to take Casey's place. Actually, that little stunt worked out even better than I'd hoped. But I have no motive. Rayne is alive. I didn't touch her. As for Casey, Rayne administered the pills, not me." He smirked.

"So, you feel nothing about Casey's death? You were in love with her."

"That was a bit of a bother. We could have had a good life together. But she rejected me." He shrugged.

Anne realized she was staring into the face of a monster. "Well, the thing is, you have motive. And today I realized what it is."

"Do tell."

"The biggest motive of all. You see, today we got married, and these words were uttered, 'I endow thee with all my worldly goods.' The focus had been on the insurance policies. In case one of you died. But what happens if one is free while the other one is locked away? Access. I'm sure when the police look into it, all of Rayne's money, her savings, IRAs, all her accounts will have been looted."

He shrugged. "Wouldn't know about that."

"Well, you'll have plenty of time to think about it when you're under arrest for the murder of Casey Judson."

"I didn't murder her."

Anne shrugged. "I wouldn't know about that."

Another group of police came over and took him into custody.

"What do you think?" Carson glanced down at Anne.

"I'm sure that once they start putting his picture up, others will come forward to say he cheated them out of their money. I don't think he meant this to go as far as it did. Sadly, Casey lost her life over it. Her rejection bruised his ego enough for him to think of her as disposable. It also doesn't put Rayne into the clear as she was the one who doped Casey, though unaware of the extra pills. Do you think she'll do time?"

"Remains to be seen. It depends on how good her

lawyers are, I suppose." Suddenly, Carson burst out laughing. "It's never a dull moment with you, N.D."

She chuckled. "It has been a crazy day, hasn't it?"

A flurry of activity caught their attention. Kandi, Stewart, Hope, Mr. and Mrs. Cole, and some of the wedding party ran toward the pair. "Did you get him?"

Anne nodded. "Yes, he's in custody now." She glanced down to see two pieces of luggage. "What's this?"

"You're already at the airport. You have your passports?"

"Yes." Carson pulled them from his pocket.

"How in the world?"

"I had planned to whisk you away after the wedding."

"To where? Are you all nuts?"

"You're like me. A planner. Kandi convinced me we needed to start our marriage by breaking the mold."

"I happen to like the mold, thank you very much," Anne replied.

Kandi grinned. "It's time for adventure. No planning. Just go!"

Carson took Anne's hand, "What do you say?"

"I...I—"

"Hold on. Be back in a jiff." He jogged over to the TSA agent, who ushered him down the hall. When Carson returned, he held two tickets in his hand. "First class."

Kandi handed the bags to them, crushing them

both in an embrace.

They waved at the pair as they accepted their bags and checked in. Stares and congratulations from onlookers were given to them as well as Kandi and Stewart.

As they made their way down the connector hall, Anne said, "Where are we going?"

"Want to turn back?"

"Nah. I'm ready for an adventure."

From the Author

Thank you for reading Duck Disaster. I hope you enjoyed it. If you did, I'd appreciate a review on what you liked about it. It helps other readers to know if the book is the right read for them.

Do you like learning about new releases, winning free books, and other giveaways? Or how about prequels or epilogues (like the one for Duck Disaster) that is only available to subscribers?

Then sign up now to my newsletter at www.vikkiwalton.com for access.

Ready for the next book in the series?

Grab Fungi Foul Play now!

Books in the Backyard Farming Series

Chicken Culprit Book 1

Cordial Killing Book 2

Honey Homicide Book 3

Christmas Capers Book 4

Potager Plot Book 5

Duck Disaster Book 6

Fungi Foul Play Book 7

Other books by Vikki Walton

Books in the Taylor Texas Mystery Series

Death Takes A Break Book 1

Death Makes A Move Book 2

Death Stakes A Claim Book 3

Death Steals A Kiss Book 4

Books in the Viviane's Adventure Series

Hijinks in Ajijic (prequel)

Deception in Devon Book 1

Made in the USA
Monee, IL
17 January 2023